# The Conjure Woman

# The Conjure Woman

## Charles W. Chesnutt

MINT EDITIONS

*The Conjure Woman* was first published in 1899.

This edition published by Mint Editions 2021.

ISBN 9781513269177 | E-ISBN 9781513274171

Published by Mint Editions®

 MINT
EDITIONS
minteditionbooks.com

Publishing Director: Jennifer Newens
Design & Production: Rachel Lopez Metzger
Typesetting: Westchester Publishing Services

# Contents

# The Goophered Grapevine

Some years ago my wife was in poor health, and our family doctor, in whose skill and honesty I had implicit confidence, advised a change of climate. I shared, from an unprofessional standpoint, his opinion that the raw winds, the chill rains, and the violent changes of temperature that characterized the winters in the region of the Great Lakes tended to aggravate my wife's difficulty, and would undoubtedly shorten her life if she remained exposed to them. The doctor's advice was that we seek, not a temporary place of sojourn, but a permanent residence, in a warmer and more equable climate. I was engaged at the time in grape-culture in northern Ohio, and, as I liked the business and had given it much study, I decided to look for some other locality suitable for carrying it on. I thought of sunny France, of sleepy Spain, of Southern California, but there were objections to them all. It occurred to me that I might find what I wanted in some one of our own Southern States. It was a sufficient time after the war for conditions in the South to have become somewhat settled; and I was enough of a pioneer to start a new industry, if I could not find a place where grape-culture had been tried. I wrote to a cousin who had gone into the turpentine business in central North Carolina. He assured me, in response to my inquiries, that no better place could be found in the South than the State and neighborhood where he lived; the climate was perfect for health, and, in conjunction with the soil, ideal for grape-culture; labor was cheap, and land could be bought for a mere song. He gave us a cordial invitation to come and visit him while we looked into the matter. We accepted the invitation, and after several days of leisurely travel, the last hundred miles of which were up a river on a sidewheel steamer, we reached our destination, a quaint old town, which I shall call Patesville, because, for one reason, that is not its name. There was a red brick market-house in the public square, with a tall tower, which held a four-faced clock that struck the hours, and from which there pealed out a curfew at nine o'clock. There were two or three hotels, a court-house, a jail, stores, offices, and all the appurtenances of a county seat and a commercial emporium; for while Patesville numbered only four or five thousand inhabitants, of all shades of complexion, it was one of the principal towns in North Carolina, and had a considerable trade in cotton and naval stores. This business activity was not immediately apparent to my unaccustomed eyes. Indeed, when I first saw the town, there brooded over it a calm that seemed almost sabbatic in its restfulness, though I learned later on that underneath its somnolent exterior the deeper currents of life—love and hatred, joy and despair, ambition and avarice, faith and friendship—flowed not less steadily than in livelier latitudes.

We found the weather delightful at that season, the end of summer, and were hospitably entertained. Our host was a man of means and evidently regarded our visit as a pleasure, and we were therefore correspondingly at our ease, and in a position to act with the coolness of judgment desirable in making so radical a change in our lives. My cousin placed a horse and buggy at our disposal, and himself acted as our guide until I became somewhat familiar with the country.

I found that grape-culture, while it had never been carried on to any great extent, was not entirely unknown in the neighborhood. Several planters thereabouts had attempted it on a commercial scale, in former years, with greater or less success; but like most Southern industries, it had felt the blight of war and had fallen into desuetude.

I went several times to look at a place that I thought might suit me. It was a plantation of considerable extent, that had formerly belonged to a wealthy man by the name of McAdoo. The estate had been for years involved in litigation between disputing heirs, during which period shiftless cultivation had well-nigh exhausted the soil. There had been a vineyard of some extent on the place, but it had not been attended to since the war, and had lapsed into utter neglect. The vines—here partly supported by decayed and broken-down trellises, there twining themselves among the branches of the slender saplings which had sprung up among them—grew in wild and unpruned luxuriance, and the few scattered grapes they bore were the undisputed prey of the first comer. The site was admirably adapted to grape-raising; the soil, with a little attention, could not have been better; and with the native grape, the luscious scuppernong, as my main reliance in the beginning, I felt sure that I could introduce and cultivate successfully a number of other varieties.

One day I went over with my wife to show her the place. We drove out of the town over a long wooden bridge that spanned a spreading mill-pond, passed the long whitewashed fence surrounding the county fair-ground, and struck into a road so sandy that the horse's feet sank to the fetlocks. Our route lay partly up hill and partly down, for we were in the sand-hill county; we drove past cultivated farms, and then by abandoned fields grown up in scrub-oak and short-leaved pine, and once or twice through the solemn aisles of the virgin forest, where the tall pines, well-nigh meeting over the narrow road, shut out the sun, and wrapped us in cloistral solitude. Once, at a cross-roads, I was in doubt as to the turn to take, and we sat there waiting ten minutes—we had already caught some of the native infection of restfulness—for some human being to come along, who could direct us on our way. At length a little negro girl appeared, walking straight as an arrow, with a piggin full of water on her head. After a little patient investigation, necessary to overcome the child's shyness, we learned what we wished to know, and at the end of about five miles from the town reached our destination.

We drove between a pair of decayed gateposts—the gate itself had long since disappeared—and up a straight sandy lane, between two lines of rotting rail fence, partly concealed by jimson-weeds and briers, to the open space where a dwelling-house had once stood, evidently a spacious mansion, if we might judge from the ruined chimneys that were still standing, and the brick pillars on which the sills rested. The house itself, we had been informed, had fallen a victim to the fortunes of war.

We alighted from the buggy, walked about the yard for a while, and then wandered off into the adjoining vineyard. Upon Annie's complaining of weariness I led the way back to the yard, where a pine log, lying under a spreading elm, afforded a shady though somewhat hard seat. One end of the log was already occupied by a venerable-looking colored man. He held on his knees a hat full of grapes, over which he was smacking his lips with great gusto, and a pile of grapeskins near him indicated that the performance was no new thing. We approached him at an angle from the rear, and were close to him before he perceived us. He respectfully rose as we drew near, and was moving away, when I begged him to keep his seat.

"Don't let us disturb you," I said. "There is plenty of room for us all."

He resumed his seat with somewhat of embarrassment. While he had been standing, I had observed that he was a tall man, and, though slightly bowed by the weight of years, apparently quite vigorous. He was not entirely black, and this fact, together with the quality of his hair, which was about six inches long and very bushy, except on the top of his head, where he was quite bald, suggested a slight strain of other than negro blood. There was a shrewdness in his eyes, too, which was not altogether African, and which, as we afterwards learned from experience, was indicative of a corresponding shrewdness in his character. He went on eating the grapes, but did not seem to enjoy himself quite so well as he had apparently done before he became aware of our presence.

"Do you live around here?" I asked, anxious to put him at his ease.

"Yas, suh. I lives des ober yander, behine de nex' san'-hill, on de Lumberton plank-road."

"Do you know anything about the time when this vineyard was cultivated?"

"Lawd bless you, suh, I knows all about it. Dey ain' na'er a man in dis settlement w'at won' tell you ole Julius McAdoo 'uz bawn en raise' on dis yer same plantation. Is you de Norv'n gemman w'at's gwine ter buy de ole vimya'd?"

"I am looking at it," I replied; "but I don't know that I shall care to buy unless I can be reasonably sure of making something out of it."

"Well, suh, you is a stranger ter me, en I is a stranger ter you, en we is bofe strangers ter one anudder, but 'f I 'uz in yo' place, I wouldn' buy dis vimya'd."

"Why not?" I asked.

"Well, I dunno whe'r you b'lieves in cunj'in' er not,—some er de w'ite folks don't, er says dey don't,—but de truf er de matter is dat dis yer ole vimya'd is goophered."

"Is what?" I asked, not grasping the meaning of this unfamiliar word.

"Is goophered,—cunju'd, bewitch'."

He imparted this information with such solemn earnestness, and with such an air of confidential mystery, that I felt somewhat interested, while Annie was evidently much impressed, and drew closer to me.

"How do you know it is bewitched?" I asked.

"I wouldn' spec' fer you ter b'lieve me 'less you know all 'bout de fac's. But ef you en young miss dere doan' min' lis'nin' ter a ole nigger run on a minute er two w'ile you er restin', I kin 'splain to you how it all happen'."

We assured him that we would be glad to hear how it all happened, and he began to tell us. At first the current of his memory—or imagination—seemed somewhat sluggish; but as his embarrassment wore off, his language flowed more freely, and the story acquired perspective and coherence. As he became more and more absorbed in the narrative, his eyes assumed a dreamy expression, and he seemed to

CHARLES W. CHESNUTT

lose sight of his auditors, and to be living over again in monologue his life on the old plantation.

"Ole Mars Dugal' McAdoo," he began, "bought dis place long many years befo' de wah, en I'member well w'en he sot out all dis yer part er de plantation in scuppernon's. De vimes growed monst'us fas', en Mars Dugal' made a thousan' gallon er scuppernon' wine eve'y year.

"Now, ef dey's an'thing a nigger lub, nex' ter 'possum, en chick'n, en watermillyums, it's scuppernon's. Dey ain' nuffin dat kin stan' up side'n de scuppernon' fer sweetness; sugar ain't a suckumstance ter scuppernon'. W'en de season is nigh 'bout ober, en de grapes begin ter swivel up des a little wid de wrinkles er ole age,—w'en de skin git sof' en brown,—den de scuppernon' make you smack yo' lip en roll yo' eye en wush fer mo'; so I reckon it ain' very 'stonishin' dat niggers lub scuppernon'.

"Dey wuz a sight er niggers in de naberhood er de vimya'd. Dere wuz ole Mars Henry Brayboy's niggers, en ole Mars Jeems McLean's niggers, en Mars Dugal's own niggers; den dey wuz a settlement er free niggers en po' buckrahs down by de Wim'l'ton Road, en Mars Dugal' had de only vimya'd in de naberhood. I reckon it ain' so much so nowadays, but befo' de wah, in slab'ry times, a nigger did n' mine goin' fi' er ten mile in a night, w'en dey wuz sump'n good ter eat at de yuther een'.

"So atter a w'ile Mars Dugal' begin ter miss his scuppernon's. Co'se he 'cuse' de niggers er it, but dey all 'nied it ter de las'. Mars Dugal' sot spring guns en steel traps, en he en de oberseah sot up nights once't er twice't, tel one night Mars Dugal'—he 'uz a monst'us keerless man— got his leg shot full er cow-peas. But somehow er nudder dey could n' nebber ketch none er de niggers. I dunner how it happen, but it happen des like I tell you, en de grapes kep' on a-goin' des de same.

"But bimeby ole Mars Dugal' fix' up a plan ter stop it. Dey wuz a cunjuh 'oman livin' down 'mongs' de free niggers on de Wim'l'ton Road, en all de darkies fum Rockfish ter Beaver Crick wuz feared er her. She could wuk de mos' powerfulles' kin' er goopher,—could make people hab fits, er rheumatiz, er make 'em des dwinel away en die; en dey say she went out ridin' de niggers at night, fer she wuz a witch 'sides bein' a cunjuh 'oman. Mars Dugal' hearn 'bout Aun' Peggy's doin's, en begun ter 'flect whe'r er no he could n' git her ter he'p him keep de niggers off'n de grapevimes. One day in de spring er de year, ole miss pack' up a basket er chick'n en poun'-cake, en a bottle er scuppernon' wine, en Mars Dugal' tuk it in his buggy en driv ober ter Aun' Peggy's cabin. He tuk de basket in, en had a long talk wid Aun' Peggy.

"De nex' day Aun' Peggy come up ter de vimya'd. De niggers seed her slippin' 'roun', en dey soon foun' out what she 'uz doin' dere. Mars Dugal' had hi'ed her ter goopher de grapevimes. She sa'ntered 'roun' 'mongs' de vimes, en tuk a leaf fum dis one, en a grape-hull fum dat one, en a grape-seed fum anudder one; en den a little twig fum here, en a little pinch er dirt fum dere,—en put it all in a big black bottle, wid a snake's toof en a speckle' hen's gall en some ha'rs fum a black cat's tail, en den fill' de bottle wid scuppernon' wine. Wen she got de goopher all ready en fix', she tuk 'n went out in de woods en buried it under de root uv a red oak tree, en den come back en tole one er de niggers she done goopher de grapevimes, en a'er a nigger w'at eat dem grapes 'ud be sho ter die inside'n twel' mont's.

"Atter dat de niggers let de scuppernon's 'lone, en Mars Dugal' did n' hab no 'casion ter fine no mo' fault; en de season wuz mos' gone, w'en a strange gemman stop at de plantation one night ter see Mars Dugal' on some business; en his coachman, seein' de scuppernon's growin' so nice en sweet, slip 'roun' behine de smoke-house, en et all de scuppernon's he could hole. Nobody did n' notice it at de time, but dat night, on de way home, de gemman's hoss runned away en kill' de coachman. W'en we hearn de noos, Aun' Lucy, de cook, she up 'n say she seed de strange nigger eat'n' er de scuppernon's behine de smoke-house; en den we knowed de goopher had b'en er wukkin'. Den one er de nigger chilluns runned away fum de quarters one day, en got in de scuppernon's, en died de nex' week. W'ite folks say he die' er de fevuh, but de niggers knowed it wuz de goopher. So you k'n be sho de darkies did n' hab much ter do wid dem scuppernon' vimes.

"W'en de scuppernon' season 'uz ober fer dat year, Mars Dugal' foun' he had made fifteen hund'ed gallon er wine; en one er de niggers hearn him laffin' wid de oberseah fit ter kill, en sayin' dem fifteen hund'ed gallon er wine wuz monst'us good intrus' on de ten dollars he laid out on de vimya'd. So I 'low ez he paid Aun' Peggy ten dollars fer to goopher de grapevimes.

"De goopher did n' wuk no mo' tel de nex' summer, w'en 'long to'ds de middle er de season one er de fiel' han's died; en ez dat lef' Mars Dugal' sho't er han's, he went off ter town fer ter buy anudder. He fotch de noo nigger home wid 'im. He wuz er ole nigger, er de color er a gingy-cake, en ball ez a hoss-apple on de top er his head. He wuz a peart ole nigger, do', en could do a big day's wuk.

"Now it happen dat one er de niggers on de nex' plantation, one er ole Mars Henry Brayboy's niggers, had runned away de day befo', en tuk ter de swamp, en ole Mars Dugal' en some er de yuther nabor w'ite folks had gone out wid dere guns en dere dogs fer ter he'p 'em hunt fer de nigger; en de han's on our own plantation wuz all so flusterated dat we fuhgot ter tell de noo han' 'bout de goopher on de scuppernon' vimes. Co'se he smell de grapes en see de vimes, an atter dahk de fus' thing he done wuz ter slip off ter de grapevimes 'dout sayin' nuffin ter nobody. Nex' mawnin' he tole some er de niggers 'bout de fine bait er scuppernon' he et de night befo'.

"Wen dey tole 'im 'bout de goopher on de grapevimes, he 'uz dat tarrified dat he turn pale, en look des like he gwine ter die right in his tracks. De oberseah come up en axed w'at 'uz de matter; en w'en dey tole 'im Henry be'n eatin' er de scuppernon's, en got de goopher on 'im, he gin Henry a big drink er w'iskey, en 'low dat de nex' rainy day he take 'im ober ter Aun' Peggy's, en see ef she would n' take de goopher off'n him, seein' ez he did n' know nuffin erbout it tel he done et de grapes.

"Sho nuff, it rain de nex' day, en de oberseah went ober ter Aun' Peggy's wid Henry. En Aun' Peggy say dat bein' ez Henry did n' know 'bout de goopher, en et de grapes in ign'ance er de conseq'ences, she reckon she mought be able fer ter take de goopher off'n him. So she fotch out er bottle wid some cunjuh medicine in it, en po'd some out in a go'd fer Henry ter drink. He manage ter git it down; he say it tas'e like whiskey wid sump'n bitter in it. She 'lowed dat 'ud keep de goopher off'n him tel de spring; but w'en de sap begin ter rise in de grapevimes he ha' ter come en see her ag'in, en she tell him w'at e's ter do.

"Nex' spring, w'en de sap commence' ter rise in de scuppernon' vime, Henry tuk a ham one night. Whar'd he git de ham? *I* doan know; dey wa'n't no hams on de plantation 'cep'n' w'at 'uz in de smoke-house, but *I* never see Henry 'bout de smoke-house. But ez I wuz a-sayin', he tuk de ham ober ter Aun' Peggy's; en Aun' Peggy tole 'im dat w'en Mars Dugal' begin ter prune de grapevimes, he mus' go en take 'n scrape off de sap whar it ooze out'n de cut een's er de vimes, en 'n'int his ball head wid it; en ef he do dat once't a year de goopher would n' wuk agin 'im long ez he done it. En bein' ez he fotch her de ham, she fix' it so he kin eat all de scuppernon' he want.

"So Henry 'n'int his head wid de sap out'n de big grapevime des ha'f way 'twix' de quarters en de big house, en de goopher nebber wuk agin him dat summer. But de beatenes' thing you eber see happen ter Henry.

Up ter dat time he wuz ez ball ez a sweeten' 'tater, but des ez soon ez de young leaves begun ter come out on de grapevimes, de ha'r begun ter grow out on Henry's head, en by de middle er de summer he had de bigges' head er ha'r on de plantation. Befo' dat, Henry had tol'able good ha'r 'roun' de aidges, but soon ez de young grapes begun ter come, Henry's ha'r begun to quirl all up in little balls, des like dis yer reg'lar grapy ha'r, en by de time de grapes got ripe his head look des like a bunch er grapes. Combin' it did n' do no good; he wuk at it ha'f de night wid er Jim Crow*, en think he git it straighten' out, but in de mawnin' de grapes 'ud be dere des de same. So he gin it up, en tried ter keep de grapes down by havin' his ha'r cut sho't.

"But dat wa'n't de quares' thing 'bout de goopher. When Henry come ter de plantation, he wuz gittin' a little ole an stiff in de j'ints. But dat summer he got des ez spry en libely ez any young nigger on de plantation; fac', he got so biggity dat Mars Jackson, de oberseah, ha' ter th'eaten ter whip 'im, ef he did n' stop cuttin' up his didos en behave hisse'f. But de mos' cur'ouses' thing happen' in de fall, when de sap begin ter go down in de grapevimes. Fus', when de grapes 'uz gethered, de knots begun ter straighten out'n Henry's ha'r; en w'en de leaves begin ter fall, Henry's ha'r 'mence' ter drap out; en when de vimes 'uz bar', Henry's head wuz baller 'n it wuz in de spring, en he begin ter git ole en stiff in de j'ints ag'in, en paid no mo' 'tention ter de gals dyoin' er de whole winter. En nex' spring, w'en he rub de sap on ag'in, he got young ag'in, en so soopl en libely dat none er de young niggers on de plantation could n' jump, ner dance, ner hoe ez much cotton ez Henry. But in de fall er de year his grapes 'mence' ter straighten out, en his j'ints ter git stiff, en his ha'r drap off, en de rheumatiz begin ter wrastle wid 'im.

"Now, ef you 'd 'a' knowed ole Mars Dugal' McAdoo, you 'd 'a' knowed dat it ha' ter be a mighty rainy day when he could n' fine sump'n fer his niggers ter do, en it ha' ter be a mighty little hole he could n' crawl thoo, en ha' ter be a monst'us cloudy night when a dollar git by him in de dahkness; en w'en he see how Henry git young in de spring en ole in de fall, he 'lowed ter hisse'f ez how he could make mo' money out'n Henry dan by wukkin' him in de cotton-fiel'. 'Long de nex' spring, atter de sap 'mence' ter rise, en Henry 'n'int 'is head en sta'ted fer ter git young en soopl, Mars Dugal' up 'n tuk Henry ter town, en sole 'im fer

---

* A small card, resembling a currycomb in construction, and used by negroes in the rural districts instead of a comb.

fifteen hunder' dollars. Co'se de man w'at bought Henry did n' know nuffin 'bout de goopher, en Mars Dugal' did n' see no 'casion fer ter tell 'im. Long to'ds de fall, w'en de sap went down, Henry begin ter git ole ag'in same ez yuzhal, en his noo marster begin ter git skeered les'n he gwine ter lose his fifteen-hunder'-dollar nigger. He sent fer a mighty fine doctor, but de med'cine did n' 'pear ter do no good; de goopher had a good holt. Henry tole de doctor 'bout de goopher, but de doctor des laff at 'im.

"One day in de winter Mars Dugal' went ter town, en wuz santerin' 'long de Main Street, when who should he meet but Henry's noo marster. Dey said 'Hoddy,' en Mars Dugal' ax 'im ter hab a seegyar; en atter dey run on awhile 'bout de craps en de weather, Mars Dugal' ax 'im, sorter keerless, like ez ef he des thought of it,—

"'How you like de nigger I sole you las' spring?'

"Henry's marster shuck his head en knock de ashes off'n his seegyar.

"'Spec' I made a bad bahgin when I bought dat nigger. Henry done good wuk all de summer, but sence de fall set in he 'pears ter be sorter pinin' away. Dey ain' nuffin pertickler de matter wid 'im—leastways de doctor say so—'cep'n' a tech er de rheumatiz; but his ha'r is all fell out, en ef he don't pick up his strenk mighty soon, I spec' I'm gwine ter lose 'im.'

"Dey smoked on awhile, en bimeby ole mars say, 'Well, a bahgin 's a bahgin, but you en me is good fren's, en I doan wan' ter see you lose all de money you paid fer dat nigger; en ef w'at you say is so, en I ain't 'sputin' it, he ain't wuf much now. I 'spec's you wukked him too ha'd dis summer, er e'se de swamps down here don't agree wid de san'-hill nigger. So you des lemme know, en ef he gits any wusser I'll be willin' ter gib yer five hund'ed dollars fer 'im, en take my chances on his livin'.'

"Sho 'nuff, when Henry begun ter draw up wid de rheumatiz en it look like he gwine ter die fer sho, his noo marster sen' fer Mars Dugal', en Mars Dugal' gin him what he promus, en brung Henry home ag'in. He tuk good keer uv 'im dyoin' er de winter,—give 'im w'iskey ter rub his rheumatiz, en terbacker ter smoke, en all he want ter eat,—'caze a nigger w'at he could make a thousan' dollars a year off'n did n' grow on eve'y huckleberry bush.

"Nex' spring, w'en de sap ris en Henry's ha'r commence' ter sprout, Mars Dugal' sole 'im ag'in, down in Robeson County dis time; en he kep' dat sellin' business up fer five year er mo'. Henry nebber say nuffin 'bout de goopher ter his noo marsters, 'caze he know he gwine ter be tuk good keer uv de nex' winter, w'en Mars Dugal' buy him back. En Mars Dugal' made 'nuff money off'n Henry ter buy anudder plantation ober on Beaver Crick.

"But 'long 'bout de een' er dat five year dey come a stranger ter stop at de plantation. De fus' day he 'uz dere he went out wid Mars Dugal' en spent all de mawnin' lookin' ober de vimya'd, en atter dinner dey spent all de evenin' playin' kya'ds. De niggers soon 'skiver' dat he wuz a Yankee, en dat he come down ter Norf C'lina fer ter l'arn de w'ite folks how to raise grapes en make wine. He promus Mars Dugal' he c'd make de grapevimes b'ar twice't ez many grapes, en dat de noo winepress he wuz a-sellin' would make mo' d'n twice't ez many gallons er wine. En ole Mars Dugal' des drunk it all in, des 'peared ter be bewitch' wid dat Yankee. Wen de darkies see dat Yankee runnin' 'roun' de vimya'd en diggin' under de grapevimes, dey shuk dere heads, en 'lowed dat dey feared Mars Dugal' losin' his min'. Mars Dugal' had all de dirt dug away fum under de roots er all de scuppernon' vimes, an' let 'em stan' dat away fer a week er mo'. Den dat Yankee made de niggers fix up a mixtry er lime en ashes en manyo, en po' it 'roun' de roots er de grapevimes. Den he 'vise Mars Dugal' fer ter trim de vimes close't, en Mars Dugal' tuck'n done eve'ything de Yankee tole him ter do. Dyoin' all er dis time, mind yer, dis yer Yankee wuz libbin' off'n de fat er de lan', at de big house, en playin' kya'ds wid Mars Dugal' eve'y night; en dey say Mars Dugal' los' mo'n a thousan' dollars dyoin' er de week dat Yankee wuz a-ruinin' de grapevimes.

"Wen de sap ris nex' spring, ole Henry 'n'inted his head ez yuzhal, en his ha'r 'mence' ter grow des de same ez it done eve'y year. De scuppernon' vimes growed monst's fas', en de leaves wuz greener en thicker dan dey eber be'n dyoin' my rememb'ance; en Henry's ha'r growed out thicker dan eber, en he 'peared ter git younger 'n younger, en soopler 'n soopler; en seein' ez he wuz sho't er ban's dat spring, havin' tuk in consid'able noo groun', Mars Dugal' 'eluded he would n' sell Henry 'tel he git de crap in en de cotton chop'. So he kep' Henry on de plantation.

"But 'long 'bout time fer de grapes ter come on de scuppernon' vimes, dey 'peared ter come a change ober 'em; de leaves withered en swivel' up, en de young grapes turn' yaller, en bimeby eve'ybody on de plantation could see dat de whole vimya'd wuz dyin'. Mars Dugal' tuk'n water de vimes en done all he could, but 't wa'n' no use: dat Yankee had done bus' de watermillyum. One time de vimes picked up a bit, en Mars Dugal' 'lowed dey wuz gwine ter come out ag'in; but dat Yankee done dug too

CHARLES W. CHESNUTT

close under de roots, en prune de branches too close ter de vime, en all dat lime en ashes done burn' de life out'n de vimes, en dey des kep' a-with'in' en a-swivelin'.

"All dis time de goopher wuz a-wukkin'. When de vimes sta'ted ter wither, Henry 'mence' ter complain er his rheumatiz; en when de leaves begin ter dry up, his ha'r 'mence' ter drap out. When de vimes fresh' up a bit, Henry'd git peart ag'in, en when de vimes wither' ag'in, Henry'd git ole ag'in, en des kep' gittin' mo' en mo' fitten fer nuffin; he des pined away, en pined away, en fine'ly tuk ter his cabin; en when de big vime whar he got de sap ter 'n'int his head withered en turned yaller en died, Henry died too,—des went out sorter like a cannel. Dey didn't 'pear ter be nuffin de matter wid 'im, 'cep'n' de rheumatiz, but his strenk des dwinel' away 'tel he did n' hab ernuff lef ter draw his bref. De goopher had got de under holt, en th'owed Henry dat time fer good en all.

"Mars Dugal' tuk on might'ly 'bout losin' his vimes en his nigger in de same year; en he swo' dat ef he could git holt er dat Yankee he'd wear 'im ter a frazzle, en den chaw up de frazzle; en he'd done it, too, for Mars Dugal' 'uz a monst'us brash man w'en he once git started. He sot de vimya'd out ober ag'in, but it wuz th'ee er fo' year befo' de vimes got ter b'arin' any scuppernon's.

"W'en de wah broke out, Mars Dugal' raise' a comp'ny, en went off ter fight de Yankees. He say he wuz mighty glad dat wah come, en he des want ter kill a Yankee fer eve'y dollar he los' 'long er dat grape-raisin' Yankee. En I 'spec' he would 'a' done it, too, ef de Yankees had n' s'picioned sump'n, en killed him fus'. Atter de s'render ole miss move' ter town, de niggers all scattered 'way fum de plantation, en de vimya'd ain' be'n cultervated sence."

"Is that story true?" asked Annie doubtfully, but seriously, as the old man concluded his narrative.

"It's des ez true ez I'm a-settin' here, miss. Dey's a easy way ter prove it: I kin lead de way right ter Henry's grave ober yander in de plantation buryin'-groun'. En I tell yer w'at, marster, I would n' 'vise you to buy dis yer ole vimya'd, 'caze de goopher 's on it yit, en dey ain' no tellin' w'en it's gwine ter crap out."

"But I thought you said all the old vines died."

"Dey did 'pear ter die, but a few un 'em come out ag'in, en is mixed in 'mongs' de yuthers. I ain' skeered ter eat de grapes, 'caze I knows de old vimes fum de noo ones; but wid strangers dey ain' no tellin' w'at mought happen. I would n' 'vise yer ter buy dis vimya'd."

I bought the vineyard, nevertheless, and it has been for a long time in a thriving condition, and is often referred to by the local press as a striking illustration of the opportunities open to Northern capital in the development of Southern industries. The luscious scuppernong holds first rank among our grapes, though we cultivate a great many other varieties, and our income from grapes packed and shipped to the Northern markets is quite considerable. I have not noticed any developments of the goopher in the vineyard, although I have a mild suspicion that our colored assistants do not suffer from want of grapes during the season.

I found, when I bought the vineyard, that Uncle Julius had occupied a cabin on the place for many years, and derived a respectable revenue from the product of the neglected grapevines. This, doubtless, accounted for his advice to me not to buy the vineyard, though whether it inspired the goopher story I am unable to state. I believe, however, that the wages I paid him for his services as coachman, for I gave him employment in that capacity, were more than an equivalent for anything he lost by the sale of the vineyard.

# Po' Sandy

On the northeast corner of my vineyard in central North Carolina, and fronting on the Lumberton plank-road, there stood a small frame house, of the simplest construction. It was built of pine lumber, and contained but one room, to which one window gave light and one door admission. Its weatherbeaten sides revealed a virgin innocence of paint. Against one end of the house, and occupying half its width, there stood a huge brick chimney: the crumbling mortar had left large cracks between the bricks; the bricks themselves had begun to scale off in large flakes, leaving the chimney sprinkled with unsightly blotches. These evidences of decay were but partially concealed by a creeping vine, which extended its slender branches hither and thither in an ambitious but futile attempt to cover the whole chimney. The wooden shutter, which had once protected the unglazed window, had fallen from its hinges, and lay rotting in the rank grass and jimson-weeds beneath. This building, I learned when I bought the place, had been used as a schoolhouse for several years prior to the breaking out of the war, since which time it had remained unoccupied, save when some stray cow or vagrant hog had sought shelter within its walls from the chill rains and nipping winds of winter.

One day my wife requested me to build her a new kitchen. The house erected by us, when we first came to live upon the vineyard, contained a very conveniently arranged kitchen; but for some occult reason my wife wanted a kitchen in the back yard, apart from the dwelling-house, after the usual Southern fashion. Of course I had to build it.

To save expense, I decided to tear down the old schoolhouse, and use the lumber, which was in a good state of preservation, in the construction of the new kitchen. Before demolishing the old house, however, I made an estimate of the amount of material contained in it, and found that I would have to buy several hundred feet of lumber additional, in order to build the new kitchen according to my wife's plan.

One morning old Julius McAdoo, our colored coachman, harnessed the gray mare to the rockaway, and drove my wife and me over to the sawmill from which I meant to order the new lumber. We drove down the long lane which led from our house to the plank-road; following the plank-road for about a mile, we turned into a road running through the forest and across the swamp to the sawmill beyond. Our carriage jolted over the half-rotted corduroy road which traversed the swamp, and then climbed the long hill leading to the sawmill. When we reached the mill, the foreman had gone over to a neighboring farmhouse, probably to smoke or gossip, and we were compelled to await his return before we could transact our business. We remained seated in the carriage, a few rods from the mill, and watched the leisurely movements of the mill-hands. We had not waited long before a huge pine log was placed in position, the machinery of the mill was set in motion, and the circular saw began to eat its way through the log, with a loud whir which resounded throughout the vicinity of the mill. The sound rose and fell in a sort of rhythmic cadence, which, heard from where we sat, was not unpleasing, and not loud enough to prevent conversation. When the saw started on its second journey through the log, Julius observed, in a lugubrious tone, and with a perceptible shudder:—

"Ugh! but dat des do cuddle my blood!"

"What's the matter, Uncle Julius?" inquired my wife, who is of a very sympathetic turn of mind. "Does the noise affect your nerves?"

"No, Mis' Annie," replied the old man, with emotion, "I ain' narvous; but dat saw, a-cuttin' en grindin' thoo dat stick er timber, en moanin', en groanin,' en sweekin', kyars my 'memb'ance back ter ole times, en 'min's me er po' Sandy." The pathetic intonation with which he lengthened out the "po' Sandy" touched a responsive chord in our own hearts.

"And who was poor Sandy?" asked my wife, who takes a deep interest in the stories of plantation life which she hears from the lips of the older colored people. Some of these stories are quaintly humorous; others wildly extravagant, revealing the Oriental cast of the negro's imagination; while others, poured freely into the sympathetic ear of a Northern-bred woman, disclose many a tragic incident of the darker side of slavery.

"Sandy," said Julius, in reply to my wife's question, "was a nigger w'at useter b'long ter ole Mars Marrabo McSwayne. Mars Marrabo's place wuz on de yuther side'n de swamp, right nex' ter yo' place. Sandy wuz a monst'us good nigger, en could do so many things erbout a plantation, en alluz 'ten' ter his wuk so well, dat w'en Mars Marrabo's chilluns growed up en married off, dey all un 'em wanted dey daddy fer ter gin 'em Sandy fer a weddin' present. But Mars Marrabo knowed de res' would n' be satisfied ef he gin Sandy ter a'er one un 'em; so w'en dey wuz all done married, he fix it by 'lowin' one er his chilluns ter take

Sandy fer a mont' er so, en den ernudder for a mont' er so, en so on dat erway tel dey had all had 'im de same lenk er time; en den dey would all take him roun' ag'in, 'cep'n' oncet in a w'ile w'en Mars Marrabo would len' 'im ter some er his yuther kinfolks 'roun' de country, w'en dey wuz short er han's; tel bimeby it got so Sandy did n' hardly knowed whar he wuz gwine ter stay fum one week's een' ter de yuther.

"One time w'en Sandy wuz lent out ez yushal, a spekilater come erlong wid a lot er niggers, en Mars Marrabo swap' Sandy's wife off fer a noo 'oman. W'en Sandy come back, Mars Marrabo gin 'im a dollar, en 'lowed he wuz monst'us sorry fer ter break up de fambly, but de spekilater had gin 'im big boot, en times wuz hard en money skase, en so he wuz bleedst ter make de trade. Sandy tuk on some 'bout losin' his wife, but he soon seed dey want no use cryin' ober spilt merlasses; en bein' ez he lacked de looks er de noo 'oman, he tuk up wid her atter she'd be'n on de plantation a mont' er so.

"Sandy en his noo wife got on mighty well tergedder, en de niggers all 'mence' ter talk about how lovin' dey wuz. Wen Tenie wuz tuk sick oncet, Sandy useter set up all night wid 'er, en den go ter wuk in de mawnin' des lack he had his reg'lar sleep; en Tenie would 'a' done anythin' in de worl' for her Sandy.

"Sandy en Tenie had n' be'n libbin' tergedder fer mo' d'n two mont's befo' Mars Marrabo's old uncle, w'at libbed down in Robeson County, sent up ter fin' out ef Mars Marrabo could n' len' 'im er hire 'im a good ban' fer a mont' er so. Sandy's marster wuz one er dese yer easy-gwine folks w'at wanter please eve'ybody, en he says yas, he could len' 'im Sandy. En Mars Marrabo tol' Sandy fer ter git ready ter go down ter Robeson nex' day, fer ter stay a mont' er so.

"It wuz monst'us hard on Sandy fer ter take 'im 'way fum Tenie. It wuz so fur down ter Robeson dat he did n' hab no chance er comin' back ter see her tel de time wuz up; he would n' 'a' mine comin' ten er fifteen mile at night ter see Tenie, but Mars Marrabo's uncle's plantation wuz mo' d'n forty mile off. Sandy wuz mighty sad en cas' down atter w'at Mars Marrabo tol' 'im, en he says ter Tenie, sezee:—

"'I'm gittin' monst'us ti'ed er dish yer gwine roun' so much. Here I is lent ter Mars Jeems dis mont', en I got ter do so-en-so; en ter Mars Archie de nex' mont', en I got ter do so-en-so; den I got ter go ter Miss Jinnie's: en hit's Sandy dis en Sandy dat, en Sandy yer en Sandy dere, tel it 'pears ter me I ain' got no home, ner no marster, ner no mistiss, ner no nuffin. I can't eben keep a wife: my yuther ole 'oman wuz sol' away widout my gittin' a chance fer ter tell her good-by; en now I got ter go off en leab you, Tenie, en I dunno whe'r I'm eber gwine ter see you ag'in er no. I wisht I wuz a tree, er a stump, er a rock, er sump'n w'at could stay on de plantation fer a w'ile.'

"Atter Sandy got thoo talkin', Tenie didn' say naer word, but des sot dere by de fier, studyin' en studyin'. Bimeby she up 'n' says:—

"'Sandy, is I eber tol' you I wuz a cunjuh 'oman?'

"Co'se Sandy had n' nebber dremp' er nuffin lack dat, en he made a great 'miration w'en he hear w'at Tenie say. Bimeby Tenie went on:—

"'I ain' goophered nobody, ner done no cunjuh wuk, fer fifteen year er mo'; en w'en I got religion I made up my mine I would n' wuk no mo' goopher. But dey is some things I doan b'lieve it's no sin fer ter do; en ef you doan wanter be sent roun' fum pillar ter pos', en ef you doan wanter go down ter Robeson, I kin fix things so you won't haf ter. Ef you'll des say de word, I kin turn you ter w'ateber you wanter be, en you kin stay right whar you wanter, ez long ez you mineter.'

"Sandy say he doan keer; he's will-in' fer ter do anythin' fer ter stay close ter Tenie. Den Tenie ax 'im ef he doan wanter be turnt inter a rabbit.

"Sandy say, 'No, de dogs mought git atter me.'

"'Shill I turn you ter a wolf?' sez Tenie.

"'No, eve'ybody 's skeered er a wolf, en I doan want nobody ter be skeered er me.'

"'Shill I turn you ter a mawkin'-bird?'

"'No, a hawk mought ketch me. I wanter be turnt inter sump'n w'at'll stay in one place.'

"'I kin turn you ter a tree,' sez Tenie. 'You won't hab no mouf ner years, but I kin turn you back oncet in a w'ile, so you kin git sump'n ter eat, en hear w'at 's gwine on.'

"Well, Sandy say dat'll do. En so Tenie tuk 'im down by de aidge er de swamp, not fur fum de quarters, en turnt 'im inter a big pine-tree, en sot 'im out 'mongs' some yuther trees. En de nex' mawnin', ez some er de fiel' han's wuz gwine long dere, dey seed a tree w'at dey did n' 'member er habbin' seed befo'; it wuz monst'us quare, en dey wuz bleedst ter 'low dat dey had n' 'membered right, er e'se one er de saplin's had be'n growin' monst'us fas'.

"W'en Mars Marrabo 'skiver' dat Sandy wuz gone, he 'lowed Sandy had runned away. He got de dogs out, but de las' place dey could track Sandy ter wuz de foot er dat pine-tree. En dere de dogs stood en barked, en bayed, en pawed at de tree, en tried ter climb up on it; en w'en dey wuz tuk roun' thoo de swamp ter look fer de scent, dey broke loose en made fer dat tree ag'in. It wuz de beatenis' thing de w'ite folks eber hearn of, en Mars Marrabo 'lowed dat Sandy must 'a' clim' up on de tree en jump' off on a mule er sump'n, en rid fur ernuff fer ter spile de scent. Mars Marrabo wanted ter 'cuse some er de yuther niggers er heppin' Sandy off, but dey all 'nied it ter de las'; en eve'ybody knowed Tenie sot too much sto' by Sandy fer ter he'p 'im run away whar she could n' nebber see 'im no mo'.

"W'en Sandy had be'n gone long ernuff fer folks ter think he done got clean away, Tenie useter go down ter de woods at night en turn 'im back, en den dey 'd slip up ter de cabin en set by de fire en talk. But dey ha' ter be monst'us keerful, er e'se somebody would 'a' seed 'em, en dat would 'a' spile' de whole thing; so Tenie alluz turnt Sandy back in de mawnin' early, befo' anybody wuz a-stirrin'.

"But Sandy did n' git erlong widout his trials en tribberlations. One day a woodpecker come erlong en 'mence' ter peck at de tree; en de nex' time Sandy wuz turnt back he had a little roun' hole in his arm, des lack a sharp stick be'n stuck in it. Atter dat Tenie sot a sparrer-hawk fer ter watch de tree; en w'en de woodpecker come erlong nex' mawnin' fer ter finish his nes', he got gobble' up mos' 'fo' he stuck his bill in de bark.

"Nudder time, Mars Marrabo sent a nigger out in de woods fer ter chop tuppentime boxes. De man chop a box in dish yer tree, en hack' de bark up two er th'ee feet, fer ter let de tuppentime run. De nex' time Sandy wuz turnt back he had a big skyar on his lef' leg, des lack it be'n skunt; en it tuk Tenie nigh 'bout all night fer ter fix a mixtry ter kyo it up. Atter dat, Tenie sot a hawnet fer ter watch de tree; en w'en de nigger come back ag'in fer ter cut ernudder box on de yuther side'n de tree, de hawnet stung 'im so hard dat de ax slip en cut his foot nigh 'bout off.

"W'en Tenie see so many things happenin' ter de tree, she 'eluded she 'd ha' ter turn Sandy ter sump'n e'se; en atter studyin' de matter ober, en talkin' wid Sandy one ebenin', she made up her mine fer ter fix up a goopher mixtry w'at would turn herse'f en Sandy ter foxes, er sump'n, so dey could run away en go some'rs whar dey could be free en lib lack w'ite folks.

"But dey ain' no tellin' w'at's gwine ter happen in dis worl'. Tenie had got de night sot fer her en Sandy ter run away, w'en dat ve'y day one er Mars Marrabo's sons rid up ter de big house in his buggy, en say his wife wuz monst'us sick, en he want his mammy ter len' 'im a 'oman fer ter nuss his wife. Tenie's mistiss say sen' Tenie; she wuz a good nuss. Young mars wuz in a tarrible hurry fer ter git back home. Tenie wuz washin' at de big house dat day, en her mistiss say she should go right 'long wid her young marster. Tenie tried ter make some 'scuse fer ter git away en hide 'tel night, w'en she would have eve'ything fix' up fer her en Sandy; she say she wanter go ter her cabin fer ter git her bonnet. Her mistiss say it doan matter 'bout de bonnet; her head-hank-cher wuz good ernuff. Den Tenie say she wanter git her bes' frock; her mistiss say no, she doan need no mo' frock, en w'en dat one got dirty she could git a clean one whar she wuz gwine. So Tenie had ter git in de buggy en go 'long wid young Mars Dunkin ter his plantation, w'ich wuz mo' d'n twenty mile away; en dey wa'n't no chance er her seein' Sandy no mo' 'tel she come back home. De po' gal felt monst'us bad 'bout de way things wuz gwine on, en she knowed Sandy mus' be a wond'rin' why she didn' come en turn 'im back no mo'.

"Wiles Tenie wuz away nussin' young Mars Dunkin's wife, Mars Marrabo tuk a notion fer ter buil' 'im a noo kitchen; en bein' ez he had lots er timber on his place, he begun ter look 'roun' fer a tree ter hab de lumber sawed out'n. En I dunno how it come to be so, but he happen fer ter hit on de ve'y tree w'at Sandy wuz turnt inter. Tenie wuz gone, en dey wa'n't nobody ner nuffin fer ter watch de tree.

"De two men w'at cut de tree down say dey nebber had sech a time wid a tree befo': dey axes would glansh off, en did n' 'pear ter make no progress thoo de wood; en of all de creakin', en shakin', en wobblin' you eber see, dat tree done it w'en it commence' ter fall. It wuz de beatenis' thing!

"W'en dey got de tree all trim' up, dey chain it up ter a timber waggin, en start fer de sawmill. But dey had a hard time gittin' de log dere: fus' dey got stuck in de mud w'en dey wuz gwine crosst de swamp, en it wuz two er th'ee hours befo' dey could git out. W'en dey start' on ag'in, de chain kep' a-comin' loose, en dey had ter keep a-stoppin' en a-stoppin' fer ter hitch de log up ag'in. W'en dey commence' ter climb de hill ter de sawmill, de log broke loose, en roll down de hill en in 'mongs' de trees, en hit tuk nigh 'bout half a day mo' ter git it haul' up ter de sawmill.

"De nex' mawnin' atter de day de tree wuz haul' ter de sawmill, Tenie come home. W'en she got back ter her cabin, de fus' thing she done wuz ter run down ter de woods en see how Sandy wuz gittin' on. Wen she seed de stump standin' dere, wid de sap runnin' out'n it, en de limbs

CHARLES W. CHESNUTT

layin' scattered roun', she nigh 'bout went out'n her min'. She run ter her cabin, en got her goopher mixtry, en den follered de track er de timber waggin ter de sawmill. She knowed Sandy could n' lib mo' d'n a minute er so ef she turnt him back, fer he wuz all chop' up so he'd 'a' be'n bleedst ter die. But she wanted ter turn 'im back long ernuff fer ter 'splain ter 'im dat she had n' went off a-purpose, en lef' 'im ter be chop' down en sawed up. She did n' want Sandy ter die wid no hard feelin's to'ds her.

"De han's at de sawmill had des got de big log on de kerridge, en wuz start-in' up de saw, w'en dey seed a 'oman runnin' up de hill, all out er bref, cryin' en gwine on des lack she wuz plumb 'stracted. It wuz Tenie; she come right inter de mill, en th'owed herse'f on de log, right in front er de saw, a-hollerin' en cryin' ter her Sandy ter fergib her, en not ter think hard er her, fer it wa'n't no fault er hern. Den Tenie 'membered de tree did n' hab no years, en she wuz gittin' ready fer ter wuk her goopher mixtry so ez ter turn Sandy back, w'en de mill-hands kotch holt er her en tied her arms wid a rope, en fasten' her to one er de posts in de sawmill; en den dey started de saw up ag'in, en cut de log up inter bo'ds en scantlin's right befo' her eyes. But it wuz mighty hard wuk; fer of all de sweekin', en moanin', en groanin', dat log done it w'iles de saw wuz a-cuttin' thoo it. De saw wuz one er dese yer ole-timey, up-en-down saws, en hit tuk longer dem days ter saw a log 'en it do now. Dey greased de saw, but dat did n' stop de fuss; hit kep' right on, tel fin'ly dey got de log all sawed up.

"W'en de oberseah w'at run de sawmill come fum breakfas', de han's up en tell him 'bout de crazy 'oman—ez dey s'posed she wuz—w'at had come runnin' in de sawmill, a-hollerin' en gwine on, en tried ter th'ow herse'f befo' de saw. En de oberseah sent two er th'ee er de han's fer ter take Tenie back ter her marster's plantation.

"Tenie 'peared ter be out'n her min' fer a long time, en her marster ha' ter lock her up in de smoke-'ouse 'tel she got ober her spells. Mars Marrabo wuz monst'us mad, en hit would 'a' made yo' flesh crawl fer ter hear him cuss, 'caze he say de spekilater w'at he got Tenie fum had fooled 'im by wukkin' a crazy 'oman off on him. Wiles Tenie wuz lock up in de smoke-'ouse, Mars Marrabo tuk 'n' haul de lumber fum de sawmill, en put up his noo kitchen.

"Wen Tenie got quiet' down, so she could be 'lowed ter go 'roun' de plantation, she up'n' tole her marster all erbout Sandy en de pine-tree; en w'en Mars Marrabo hearn it, he 'lowed she wuz de wuss 'stracted nigger he eber hearn of. He did n' know w'at ter do wid Tenie: fus' he thought he 'd put her in de po'house; but fin'ly, seein' ez she did n' do no harm ter nobody ner nuffin, but des went 'roun' moanin', en groanin', en shakin' her head, he 'cluded ter let her stay on de plantation en nuss de little nigger chilluns w'en dey mammies wuz ter wuk in de cotton-fiel'.

"De noo kitchen Mars Marrabo buil' wuz n' much use, fer it had n' be'n put up long befo' de niggers 'mence' ter notice quare things erbout it. Dey could hear sump'n moanin' en groanin' 'bout de kitchen in de night-time, en w'en de win' would blow dey could hear sump'n a-hollerin' en sweekin' lack it wuz in great pain en sufferin'. En it got so atter a w'ile dat it wuz all Mars Marrabo's wife could do ter git a 'oman ter stay in de kitchen in de daytime long ernuff ter do de cookin'; en dey wa'n't naer nigger on de plantation w'at would n' rudder take forty dan ter go 'bout dat kitchen atter dark,—dat is, 'cep'n' Tenie; she did n' 'pear ter min' de ha'nts. She useter slip 'roun' at night, en set on de kitchen steps, en lean up agin de do'-jamb, en run on ter herse'f wid some kine er foolishness w'at nobody could n' make out; fer Mars Marrabo had th'eaten' ter sen' her off'n de plantation ef she say anything ter any er de yuther niggers 'bout de pine-tree. But somehow er 'nudder de niggers foun' out all erbout it, en dey all knowed de kitchen wuz ha'nted by Sandy's sperrit. En bimeby hit got so Mars Marrabo's wife herse'f wuz skeered ter go out in de yard atter dark.

"Wen it come ter dat, Mars Marrabo tuk en to' de kitchen down, en use' de lumber fer ter buil' dat ole school'ouse w'at you er talkin' 'bout pullin' down. De school'ouse wuz n' use' 'cep'n' in de daytime, en on dark nights folks gwine 'long de road would hear quare soun's en see quare things. Po' ole Tenie useter go down dere at night, en wander 'roun' de school'ouse; en de niggers all 'lowed she went fer ter talk wid Sandy's sperrit. En one winter mawnin', w'en one er de boys went ter school early fer ter start de fire, w'at should he fin' but po' ole Tenie, layin' on de flo', stiff, en col', en dead. Dere did n' 'pear ter be nuffin pertickler de matter wid her,—she had des grieve' herse'f ter def fer her Sandy. Mars Marrabo didn' shed no tears. He thought Tenie wuz crazy, en dey wa'n't no tellin' w'at she mought do nex'; en dey ain' much room in dis worl' fer crazy w'ite folks, let 'lone a crazy nigger.

"Hit wa'n't long atter dat befo' Mars Marrabo sol' a piece er his track er lan' ter Mars Dugal' McAdoo,—*my* ole marster,—en dat 's how de ole school'ouse happen to be on yo' place. Wen de wah broke out, de school stop', en de ole school'ouse be'n stannin' empty ever sence,—dat is, 'cep'n' fer de ha'nts. En folks sez dat de ole school'ouse, er any yuther house w'at got any er dat lumber in it w'at wuz sawed out'n de tree w'at Sandy wuz turnt inter, is gwine ter be ha'nted tel de las' piece er plank is rotted en crumble' inter dus'."

Annie had listened to this gruesome narrative with strained attention.

"What a system it was," she exclaimed, when Julius had finished, "under which such things were possible!"

"What things?" I asked, in amazement. "Are you seriously considering the possibility of a man's being turned into a tree?"

"Oh, no," she replied quickly, "not that;" and then she murmured absently, and with a dim look in her fine eyes, "Poor Tenie!"

We ordered the lumber, and returned home. That night, after we had gone to bed, and my wife had to all appearances been sound asleep for half an hour, she startled me out of an incipient doze by exclaiming suddenly,—

"John, I don't believe I want my new kitchen built out of the lumber in that old schoolhouse."

"You wouldn't for a moment allow yourself," I replied, with some asperity, "to be influenced by that absurdly impossible yarn which Julius was spinning to-day?"

"I know the story is absurd," she replied dreamily, "and I am not so silly as to believe it. But I don't think I should ever be able to take any pleasure in that kitchen if it were built out of that lumber. Besides, I think the kitchen would look better and last longer if the lumber were all new."

Of course she had her way. I bought the new lumber, though not without grumbling. A week or two later I was called away from home on business. On my return, after an absence of several days, my wife remarked to me,—

"John, there has been a split in the Sandy Run Colored Baptist Church, on the temperance question. About half the members have come out from the main body, and set up for themselves. Uncle Julius is one of the seceders, and he came to me yesterday and asked if they might not hold their meetings in the old schoolhouse for the present."

"I hope you didn't let the old rascal have it," I returned, with some warmth. I had just received a bill for the new lumber I had bought.

"Well," she replied, "I couldn't refuse him the use of the house for so good a purpose."

"And I'll venture to say," I continued, "that you subscribed something toward the support of the new church?"

She did not attempt to deny it.

"What are they going to do about the ghost?" I asked, somewhat curious to know how Julius would get around this obstacle.

"Oh," replied Annie, "Uncle Julius says that ghosts never disturb religious worship, but that if Sandy's spirit *should* happen to stray into meeting by mistake, no doubt the preaching would do it good."

# MARS JEEMS'S NIGHTMARE

We found old Julius very useful when we moved to our new residence. He had a thorough knowledge of the neighborhood, was familiar with the roads and the watercourses, knew the qualities of the various soils and what they would produce, and where the best hunting and fishing were to be had. He was a marvelous hand in the management of horses and dogs, with whose mental processes he manifested a greater familiarity than mere use would seem to account for, though it was doubtless due to the simplicity of a life that had kept him close to nature. Toward my tract of land and the things that were on it—the creeks, the swamps, the hills, the meadows, the stones, the trees—he maintained a peculiar personal attitude, that might be called predial rather than proprietary. He had been accustomed, until long after middle life, to look upon himself as the property of another. When this relation was no longer possible, owing to the war, and to his master's death and the dispersion of the family, he had been unable to break off entirely the mental habits of a lifetime, but had attached himself to the old plantation, of which he seemed to consider himself an appurtenance. We found him useful in many ways and entertaining in others, and my wife and I took quite a fancy to him.

Shortly after we became established in our home on the sand-hills, Julius brought up to the house one day a colored boy of about seventeen, whom he introduced as his grandson, and for whom he solicited employment. I was not favorably impressed by the youth's appearance,—quite the contrary, in fact; but mainly to please the old man I hired Tom—his name was Tom—to help about the stables, weed the garden, cut wood and bring water, and in general to make himself useful about the outdoor work of the household.

My first impression of Tom proved to be correct. He turned out to be very trifling, and I was much annoyed by his laziness, his carelessness, and his apparent lack of any sense of responsibility. I kept him longer than I should, on Julius's account, hoping that he might improve; but he seemed to grow worse instead of better, and when I finally reached the limit of my patience, I discharged him.

"I am sorry, Julius," I said to the old man; "I should have liked to oblige you by keeping him; but I can't stand Tom any longer. He is absolutely untrustworthy."

"Yas, suh," replied Julius, with a deep sigh and a long shake of the head, "I knows he ain' much account, en dey ain' much 'pen'ence ter be put on 'im. But I wuz hopin' dat you mought make some 'lowance fuh a' ign'ant young nigger, suh, en gib 'im one mo' chance."

But I had hardened my heart. I had always been too easily imposed upon, and had suffered too much from this weakness. I determined to be firm as a rock in this instance.

"No, Julius," I rejoined decidedly, "it is impossible. I gave him more than a fair trial, and he simply won't do."

When my wife and I set out for our drive in the cool of the evening,—afternoon is "evening" in Southern parlance,—one of the servants put into the rock-away two large earthenware jugs. Our drive was to be down through the swamp to the mineral spring at the foot of the sand-hills beyond. The water of this spring was strongly impregnated with sulphur and iron, and, while not particularly agreeable of smell or taste, was used by us, in moderation, for sanitary reasons.

When we reached the spring, we found a man engaged in cleaning it out. In answer to an inquiry he said that if we would wait five or ten minutes, his task would be finished and the spring in such condition that we could fill our jugs. We might have driven on, and come back by way of the spring, but there was a bad stretch of road beyond, and we concluded to remain where we were until the spring should be ready. We were in a cool and shady place. It was often necessary to wait awhile in North Carolina; and our Northern energy had not been entirely proof against the influences of climate and local custom.

While we sat there, a man came suddenly around a turn of the road ahead of us. I recognized in him a neighbor with whom I had exchanged formal calls. He was driving a horse, apparently a high-spirited creature, possessing, so far as I could see at a glance, the marks of good temper and good breeding; the gentleman, I had heard it suggested, was slightly deficient in both. The horse was rearing and plunging, and the man was beating him furiously with a buggy-whip. When he saw us, he flushed a fiery red, and, as he passed, held the reins with one hand, at some risk to his safety, lifted his hat, and bowed somewhat constrainedly as the horse darted by us, still panting and snorting with fear.

"He looks as though he were ashamed of himself," I observed.

"I'm sure he ought to be," exclaimed my wife indignantly. "I think there is no worse sin and no more disgraceful thing than cruelty."

"I quite agree with you," I assented.

CHARLES W. CHESNUTT

"A man w'at 'buses his hoss is gwine ter be ha'd on de folks w'at wuks fer 'im," remarked Julius. "Ef young Mistah McLean doan min', he'll hab a bad dream one er dese days, des lack 'is grandaddy had way back yander, long yeahs befo' de wah."

"What was it about Mr. McLean's dream, Julius?" I asked. The man had not yet finished cleaning the spring, and we might as well put in time listening to Julius as in any other way. We had found some of his plantation tales quite interesting.

"Mars Jeems McLean," said Julius, "wuz de grandaddy er dis yer gent'eman w'at is des gone by us beatin' his hoss. He had a big plantation en a heap er niggers. Mars Jeems wuz a ha'd man, en monst'us stric' wid his han's. Eber sence he growed up he nebber 'peared ter hab no feelin' fer nobody. W'en his daddy, ole Mars John McLean, died, de plantation en all de niggers fell ter young Mars Jeems. He had be'n bad 'nuff befo', but it wa'n't long atterwa'ds 'tel he got so dey wuz no use in libbin' at all ef you ha' ter lib roun' Mars Jeems. His niggers wuz bleedzd ter slabe fum daylight ter da'k, w'iles yuther folks's did n' hafter wuk 'cep'n' fum sun ter sun; en dey did n' git no mo' ter eat dan dey oughter, en dat de coa'ses' kin'. Dey wa'n't 'lowed ter sing, ner dance, ner play de banjo w'en Mars Jeems wuz roun' de place; fer Mars Jeems say he would n' hab no sech gwines-on,—said he bought his han's ter wuk, en not ter play, en w'en night come dey mus' sleep en res', so dey 'd be ready ter git up soon in de mawnin' en go ter dey wuk fresh en strong.

"Mars Jeems did n' 'low no co'tin' er juneseyin' roun' his plantation,— said he wanted his niggers ter put dey min's on dey wuk, en not be wastin' dey time wid no sech foolis'ness. En he would n' let his han's git married,—said he wuz n' raisin' niggers, but wuz raisin' cotton. En w'eneber any er de boys en gals 'ud 'mence ter git sweet on one ernudder, he 'd sell one er de yuther un 'em, er sen' 'em way down in Robeson County ter his yuther plantation, whar dey could n' nebber see one ernudder.

"Ef any er de niggers eber complained, dey got fo'ty; so co'se dey did n' many un 'em complain. But dey did n' lack it, des de same, en nobody could n' blame 'em, fer dey had a ha'd time. Mars Jeems did n' make no 'lowance fer nachul bawn laz'ness, ner sickness, ner trouble in de min', ner nuffin; he wuz des gwine ter git so much wuk outer eve'y han', er know de reason w'y.

"Dey wuz one time de niggers 'lowed, fer a spell, dat Mars Jeems mought git bettah. He tuk a lackin' ter Mars Marrabo McSwayne's oldes' gal, Miss Libbie, en useter go ober dere eve'y day er eve'y ebenin', en folks said dey wuz gwine ter git married sho'. But it 'pears dat Miss Libbie heared 'bout de gwineson on Mars Jeems's plantation, en she des 'lowed she could n' trus' herse'f wid no sech a man; dat he mought git so useter 'busin' his niggers dat he 'd 'mence ter 'buse his wife atter he got useter habbin' her roun' de house. So she 'clared she wuz n' gwine ter hab nuffin mo' ter do wid young Mars Jeems.

"De niggers wuz all monst'us sorry w'en de match wuz bust' up, fer now Mars Jeems got wusser 'n he wuz befo' he sta'ted sweethea'tin'. De time he useter spen' co'tin' Miss Libbie he put in findin' fault wid de niggers, en all his bad feelin's 'ca'se Miss Libbie th'owed 'im ober he 'peared ter try ter wuk off on de po' niggers.

"W'iles Mars Jeems wuz co'tin' Miss Libbie, two er de han's on de plantation had got ter settin' a heap er sto' by one ernudder. One un 'em wuz name' Solomon, en de yuther wuz a 'oman w'at wukked in de fiel' 'long er 'im—I fe'git dat 'oman's name, but it doan 'mount ter much in de tale nohow. Now, whuther 'ca'se Mars Jeems wuz so tuk up wid his own junesey* dat he did n' paid no 'tention fer a w'ile ter w'at wuz gwine on 'twix' Solomon en his junesey, er whuther his own co'tin' made 'im kin' er easy on de co'tin' in de qua'ters, dey ain' no tellin'. But dey's one thing sho', dat w'en Miss Libbie th'owed 'im ober, he foun' out 'bout Solomon en de gal monst'us quick, en gun Solomon fo'ty, en sont de gal down ter de Robeson County plantation, en tol' all de niggers ef he ketch 'em at any mo' sech foolishness, he wuz gwine ter skin 'em alibe en tan dey hides befo' dey ve'y eyes. Co'se he would n' 'a' done it, but he mought 'a' made things wusser 'n dey wuz. So you kin 'magine dey wa'n't much lub-makin' in de qua'ters fer a long time.

"Mars Jeems useter go down ter de yuther plantation sometimes fer a week er mo', en so he had ter hab a oberseah ter look atter his wuk w'iles he 'uz gone. Mars Jeems's oberseah wuz a po' w'ite man name' Nick Johnson,—de niggers called 'im Mars Johnson ter his face, but behin' his back dey useter call 'im Ole Nick, en de name suited 'im ter a T. He wuz wusser 'n Mars Jeems ever da'ed ter be. Co'se de darkies did n' lack de way Mars Jeems used 'em, but he wuz de marster, en had a right ter do ez he please'; but dis yer Ole Nick wa'n't nuffin but a po' buckrah, en all de niggers 'spised 'im ez much ez dey hated 'im, fer he did n' own

---

* Sweetheart.

nobody, en wa'n't no bettah 'n a nigger, fer in dem days any 'spectable pusson would ruther be a nigger dan a po' w'ite man.

"Now, atter Solomon's gal had be'n sont away, he kep' feelin' mo' en mo' bad erbout it, 'tel fin'lly he 'lowed he wuz gwine ter see ef dey could n' be sump'n done fer ter git 'er back, en ter make Mars Jeems treat de darkies bettah. So he tuk a peck er co'n out'n de ba'n one night, en went ober ter see ole Aun' Peggy, de free-nigger cunjuh 'oman down by de Wim'l'ton Road.

"Aun' Peggy listen' ter 'is tale, en ax' him some queshtuns, en den tol' 'im she 'd wuk her roots, en see w'at dey 'd say 'bout it, en ter-morrer night he sh'd come back ag'in en fetch ernudder peck er co'n, en den she 'd hab sump'n fer ter tell 'im.

"So Solomon went back de nex' night, en sho' 'nuff, Aun' Peggy tol' 'im w'at ter do. She gun 'im some stuff w'at look' lack it be'n made by poundin' up some roots en yarbs wid a pestle in a mo'tar.

"'Dis yer stuff,' sez she, 'is monst'us pow'ful kin' er goopher. You take dis home, en gin it ter de cook, ef you kin trus' her, en tell her fer ter put it in yo' marster's soup de fus' cloudy day he hab okra soup fer dinnah. Min' you follers de d'rections.'

"'It ain' gwineter p'isen 'im, is it?' ax' Solomon, gittin' kin' er skeered; fer Solomon wuz a good man, en did n' want ter do nobody no rale ha'm.

"'Oh, no,' sez ole Aun' Peggy, 'it's gwine ter do 'im good, but he'll hab a monst'us bad dream fus'. A mont' fum now you come down heah en lemme know how de goopher is wukkin'. Fer I ain' done much er dis kin' er cunj'in' er late yeahs, en I has ter kinder keep track un it ter see dat it doan 'complish no mo' d'n I 'lows fer it ter do. En I has ter be kinder keerful 'bout cunj'in' w'ite folks; so be sho' en lemme know, w'ateber you do, des w'at is gwine on roun' de plantation.'

"So Solomon say all right, en tuk de goopher mixtry up ter de big house en gun it ter de cook, en tol' her fer ter put it in Mars Jeems's soup de fus' cloudy day she hab okra soup fer dinnah. It happen' dat de ve'y nex' day wuz a cloudy day, en so de cook made okra soup fer Mars Jeems's dinnah, en put de powder Solomon gun her inter de soup, en made de soup rale good, so Mars Jeems eat a whole lot of it en 'peared ter enjoy it.

"De nex' mawnin' Mars Jeems tol' de oberseah he wuz gwine 'way on some bizness, en den he wuz gwine ter his yuther plantation, down in Robeson County, en he did n' 'spec' he 'd be back fer a mont' er so.

"'But,' sezee, 'I wants you ter run dis yer plantation fer all it's wuth. Dese yer niggers is gittin' monst'us triflin' en lazy en keerless, en dey ain' no 'pen'ence ter be put in 'em. I wants dat stop', en w'iles I 'm gone erway I wants de 'spenses cut 'way down en a heap mo' wuk done. Fac', I wants dis yer plantation ter make a reco'd dat'll show w'at kinder oberseah you is.'

"Ole Nick did n' said nuffin but 'Yas, suh,' but de way he kinder grin' ter hisse'f en show' his big yaller teef, en snap' de rawhide he useter kyar roun' wid 'im, made col' chills run up and down de backbone er dem niggers w'at heared Mars Jeems a-talkin'. En dat night dey wuz mo'nin' en groanin' down in de qua'ters, fer de niggers all knowed w'at wuz comin'.

"So, sho' 'nuff, Mars Jeems went erway nex' mawnin', en de trouble begun. Mars Johnson sta'ted off de ve'y fus' day fer ter see w'at he could hab ter show Mars Jeems w'en he come back. He made de tasks bigger en de rashuns littler, en w'en de niggers had wukked all day, he 'd fin' sump'n fer 'em ter do roun' de ba'n er som'ers atter da'k, fer ter keep 'em busy a' hour er so befo' dey went ter sleep.

"About th'ee er fo' days atter Mars Jeems went erway, young Mars Dunkin McSwayne rode up ter de big house one day wid a nigger settin' behin' 'im in de buggy, tied ter de seat, en ax' ef Mars Jeems wuz home. Mars Johnson wuz at de house, and he say no.

"'Well,' sez Mars Dunkin, sezee, 'I fotch dis nigger ober ter Mistah McLean fer ter pay a bet I made wid 'im las' week w'en we wuz playin' kya'ds te'gedder. I bet 'im a nigger man, en heah 's one I reckon'll fill de bill. He wuz tuk up de yuther day fer a stray nigger, en he could n' gib no 'count er hisse'f, en so he wuz sol' at oction, en I bought 'im. He's kinder brash, but I knows yo' powers, Mistah Johnson, en I reckon ef anybody kin make 'im toe de ma'k, you is de man.'

"Mars Johnson grin' one er dem grins w'at show' all his snaggle teef, en make de niggers 'low he look lack de ole debbil, en sezee ter Mars Dunkin:—

"'I reckon you kin trus' me, Mistah Dunkin, fer ter tame any nigger wuz eber bawn. De nigger doan lib w'at I can't take down in 'bout fo' days.'

"Well, Ole Nick had 'is han's full long er dat noo nigger; en w'iles de res' er de darkies wuz sorry fer de po' man, dey 'lowed he kep' Mars Johnson so busy dat dey got along better 'n dey 'd 'a' done ef de noo nigger had nebber come.

"De fus' thing dat happen', Mars Johnson sez ter dis yer noo man:—

"'W'at 's yo' name, Sambo?'

"'My name ain' Sambo,' 'spon' de noo nigger.

"'Did I ax you w'at yo' name wa'n't?' sez Mars Johnson. 'You wants ter be pa'tic'lar how you talks ter me. Now, w'at is yo' name, en whar did you come fum?'

"'I dunno my name,' sez de nigger, 'en I doan 'member whar I come fum. My head is all kin' er mix' up.'

"'Yas,' sez Mars Johnson, 'I reckon I'll ha' ter gib you sump'n fer ter cl'ar yo' head. At de same time, it'll l'arn you some manners, en atter dis mebbe you'll say "suh" w'en you speaks ter me.'

"Well, Mars Johnson haul' off wid his rawhide en hit de noo nigger once. De noo man look' at Mars Johnson fer a minute ez ef he did n' know w'at ter make er dis yer kin' er l'arnin'. But w'en de oberseah raise' his w'ip ter hit him ag'in, de noo nigger des haul' off en made fer Mars Johnson, en ef some er de yuther niggers had n' stop' 'im, it 'peared ez ef he mought 'a' made it wa'm fer Ole Nick dere fer a w'ile. But de oberseah made de yuther niggers he'p tie de noo nigger up, en den gun 'im fo'ty, wid a dozen er so th'owed in fer good measure, fer Ole Nick wuz nebber stingy wid dem kin' er rashuns. De nigger went on at a tarrable rate, des lack a wil' man, but co'se he wuz bleedzd ter take his med'cine, fer he wuz tied up en could n' he'p his-se'f.

"Mars Johnson lock' de noo nigger up in de ba'n, en did n' gib 'im nuffin ter eat fer a day er so, 'tel he got 'im kin'er quiet' down, en den he tu'nt 'im loose en put 'im ter wuk. De nigger 'lowed he wa'n't useter wukkin', en would n' wuk, en Mars Johnson gun 'im anudder fo'ty fer laziness en impidence, en let 'im fas' a day er so mo', en den put 'im ter wuk ag'in. De nigger went ter wuk, but did n' 'pear ter know how ter han'le a hoe. It tuk des 'bout half de oberseah's time lookin' atter 'im, en dat po' nigger got mo' lashin's en cussin's en cuffin's dan any fo' yuthers on de plantation. He did n' mix' wid ner talk much ter de res' er de niggers, en could n' 'pear ter git it th'oo his min' dat he wuz a slabe en had ter wuk en min' de w'ite folks, spite er de fac' dat Ole Nick gun 'im a lesson eve'y day. En fin'lly Mars Johnson 'lowed dat he could n' do nuffin wid 'im; dat ef he wuz his nigger, he'd break his sperrit er break 'is neck, one er de yuther. But co'se he wuz only sont ober on trial, en ez he did n' gib sat'sfaction, en he had n' heared fum Mars Jeems 'bout w'en he wuz comin' back; en ez he wuz feared he'd git mad some time er 'nuther en kill de nigger befo' he knowed it, he 'lowed he'd better sen' 'im back whar he come fum. So he tied 'im up en sont 'im back ter Mars Dunkin.

"Now, Mars Dunkin McSwayne wuz one er dese yer easy-gwine gent'emen w'at did n' lack ter hab no trouble wid niggers er nobody e'se, en he knowed ef Mars Ole Nick could n' git 'long wid dis nigger, nobody could. So he tuk de nigger ter town dat same day, en sol' 'im ter a trader w'at wuz gittin' up a gang er lackly niggers fer ter ship off on de steamboat ter go down de ribber ter Wim'l'ton en fum dere ter Noo Orleens.

"De nex' day atter de noo man had be'n sont away, Solomon wuz wukkin' in de cotton-fiel', en w'en he got ter de fence nex' ter de woods, at de een' er de row, who sh'd he see on de yuther side but ole Aun' Peggy. She beckon' ter 'im,—de oberseah wuz down on de yuther side er de fiel',—en sez she:—

"'W'y ain' you done come en 'po'ted ter me lack I tol' you?'

"'W'y, law! Aun' Peggy,' sez Solomon, 'dey ain' nuffin ter 'po't. Mars Jeems went away de day atter we gun 'im de goopher mixtry, en we ain' seed hide ner hair un 'im sence, en co'se we doan know nuffin 'bout w'at 'fec' it had on 'im.'

"'I doan keer nuffin 'bout yo' Mars Jeems now; w'at I wants ter know is w'at be'n gwine on 'mongs' de niggers. Has you be'n gittin' 'long any better on de plantation?'

"'No, Aun' Peggy, we be'n gittin' 'long wusser. Mars Johnson is stric'er 'n he eber wuz befo', en de po' niggers doan ha'dly git time ter draw dey bref, en dey 'lows dey mought des ez well be dead ez alibe.'

"'Uh huh!' sez Aun' Peggy, sez she, 'I tol' you dat 'uz monst'us pow'ful goopher, en its wuk doan 'pear all at once.'

"'Long ez we had dat noo nigger heah,' Solomon went on, 'he kep' Mars Johnson busy pa't er de time; but now he 's gone erway, I s'pose de res' un us'll ketch it wusser 'n eber.'

"'W'at's gone wid de noo nigger?' sez Aun' Peggy, rale quick, battin' her eyes en straight'nin' up.

"'Ole Nick done sont 'im back ter Mars Dunkin, who had fotch 'im heah fer ter pay a gamblin' debt ter Mars Jeems,' sez Solomon, 'en I heahs Mars Dunkin has sol' 'im ter a nigger-trader up in Patesville, w'at 's gwine ter ship 'im off wid a gang ter-morrer.'

"Ole Aun' Peggy 'peared ter git rale stirred up w'en Solomon tol' 'er dat, en sez she, shakin' her stick at 'im:—

"'W'y did n' you come en tell me 'bout dis noo nigger bein' sol' erway? Did n' you promus me, ef I 'd gib you dat goopher, you 'd come en 'po't ter me 'bout all w'at wuz gwine on on dis plantation Co'se I could 'a' foun' out fer myse'f, but I 'pended on yo' tellin' me, en now by not doin' it I's feared you gwine spile my cunj'in'. You come down ter my house ter-night en do w'at I tells you, er I'll put a spell on you dat 'll make yo' ha'r fall out so you'll be bal', en yo' eyes drap out so you can't see, en yo teef fall out so you can't eat, en yo' years grow up so you can't heah. Wen you is foolin' wid a cunjuh 'oman lack me, you got ter min' yo' P's en Q's er dey'll be trouble sho' 'nuff.'

"So co'se Solomon went down ter Aun' Peggy's dat night, en she gun 'im a roasted sweet'n' 'tater.

"'You take dis yer sweet'n' 'tater,' sez she,—'I done goophered it 'speshly fer dat noo nigger, so you better not eat it yo'se'f er you'll wush you had n',—en slip off ter town, en fin' dat strange man, en gib 'im dis yer sweet'n' 'tater. He mus' eat it befo' mawnin', sho', ef he doan wanter be sol' erway ter Noo Orleens.'

"'But s'posen de patteroles ketch me, Aun' Peggy, w'at I gwine ter do?' sez Solomon.

"'De patteroles ain' gwine tech you, but ef you doan fin' dat nigger, I 'm gwine git you, en you'll fin' me wusser 'n de patteroles. Des hol' on a minute, en I'll sprinkle you wid some er dis mixtry out'n dis yer bottle, so de patteroles can't see you, en you kin rub yo' feet wid some er dis yer grease out'n dis go'd, so you kin run fas', en rub some un it on yo' eyes so you kin see in de da'k; en den you mus' fin' dat noo nigger en gib 'im dis yer 'tater, er you gwine ter hab mo' trouble on yo' ban's 'n you eber had befo' in yo' life er eber will hab sence.'

"So Solomon tuk de sweet'n' 'tater en sta'ted up de road fas' ez he could go, en befo' long he retch' town. He went right 'long by de patteroles, en dey did n' 'pear ter notice 'im, en bimeby he foun' whar de strange nigger was kep', en he walked right pas' de gyard at de do' en foun' 'im. De nigger could n' see 'im, ob co'se, en he could n' 'a' seed de nigger in de da'k, ef it had n' be'n fer de stuff Aun' Peggy gun 'im ter rub on 'is eyes. De nigger wuz layin' in a co'nder, 'sleep, en Solomon des slip' up ter 'im, en hilt dat sweet'n' 'tater 'fo' de nigger's nose, en he des nach'ly retch' up wid his han', en tuk de 'tater en eat it in his sleep, widout knowin' it. Wen Solomon seed he 'd done eat de 'tater, he went back en tol' Aun' Peggy, en den went home ter his cabin ter sleep, 'way 'long 'bout two o'clock in de mawnin'.

"De nex' day wuz Sunday, en so de niggers had a little time ter deyse'ves. Solomon wuz kinder 'sturb' in his min' thinkin' 'bout his junesey w'at 'uz gone away, en wond'rin' w'at Aun' Peggy had ter do wid dat noo nigger; en he had sa'ntered up in de woods so 's ter be by hisse'f a little, en at de same time ter look atter a rabbit-trap he'd sot down in de aidge er de swamp, w'en who sh'd he see stan'in' unner a tree but a w'ite man.

"Solomon did n' knowed de w'ite man at fus', 'tel de w'ite man spoke up ter 'im.

"'Is dat you, Solomon?' sezee.

"Den Solomon reco'nized de voice.

"'Fer de Lawd's sake, Mars Jeems! is dat you?'

"'Yas, Solomon,' sez his marster, 'dis is me, er w'at's lef er me.'

"It wa'n't no wonder Solomon had n' knowed Mars Jeems at fus', fer he wuz dress' lack a po' w'ite man, en wuz barefooted, en look' monst'us pale en peaked, ez ef he'd des come th'oo a ha'd spell er sickness.

"'You er lookin' kinder po'ly, Mars Jeems,' sez Solomon. 'Is you be'n sick, suh?'

"'No, Solomon,' sez Mars Jeems, shakin' his head, en speakin' sorter slow en sad, 'I ain' be'n sick, but I's had a monst'us bad dream,—fac', a reg'lar, nach'ul nightmare. But tell me how things has be'n gwine on up ter de plantation sence I be'n gone, Solomon.'

"So Solomon up en tol' 'im 'bout de craps, en 'bout de hosses en de mules, en 'bout de cows en de hawgs. En w'en he 'mence' ter tell 'bout de noo nigger, Mars Jeems prick' up 'is yeahs en listen', en eve'y now en den he 'd say, 'Uh huh! uh huh!' en nod 'is head. En bimeby, w'en he 'd ax' Solomon some mo' queshtuns, he sez, sezee:—

"'Now, Solomon, I doan want you ter say a wo'd ter nobody 'bout meetin' me heah, but I wants you ter slip up ter de house, en fetch me some clo's en some shoes,—I fergot ter tell you dat a man rob' me back yander on de road en swap' clo's wid me widout axin' me whuther er no,—but you neenter say nuffin 'bout dat, nuther. You go en fetch me some clo's heah, so nobody won't see you, en keep yo' mouf shet, en I 'll gib you a dollah.'

"Solomon wuz so 'stonish' he lack ter fell ober in his tracks, w'en Mars Jeems promus' ter gib 'im a dollah. Dey su't'nly wuz a change come ober Mars Jeems, w'en he offer' one er his niggers dat much money. Solomon 'mence' ter 'spec' dat Aun' Peggy's cunj'ation had be'n wukkin' monst'us strong.

"Solomon fotch Mars Jeems some clo's en shoes, en dat same eb'nin' Mars Jeems 'peared at de house, en let on lack he des dat minute got home fum Robeson County. Mars Johnson was all ready ter talk ter 'im, but Mars Jeems sont 'im wo'd he wa'n't feelin' ve'y well dat night, en he'd see 'im ter-morrer.

"So nex' mawnin' atter breakfus' Mars Jeems sont fer de oberseah, en ax' 'im fer ter gib 'count er his styoa'dship. Ole Nick tol' Mars Jeems how much wuk be'n done, en got de books en showed 'im how much money be'n save'. Den Mars Jeems ax' 'im how de darkies be'n behabin', en Mars Johnson say dey be'n behabin' good, most un 'em, en dem w'at did n' behave good at fus' change dey conduc' atter he got holt un 'em a time er two.

"'All,' sezee, "cep'n' de noo nigger Mistah Dunkin fotch ober heah en lef on trial, w'iles you wuz gone.'

"'Oh, yas,' 'lows Mars Jeems, 'tell me all 'bout dat noo nigger. I heared a little 'bout dat quare noo nigger las' night, en it wuz des too rediklus. Tell me all 'bout dat noo nigger.'

"So seein' Mars Jeems so good-na-chu'd 'bout it, Mars Johnson up en tol' 'im how he tied up de noo ban' de fus' day en gun 'im fo'ty 'ca'se he would n' tell 'im 'is name.

"'Ha, ha, ha!' sez Mars Jeems, laffin' fit ter kill, 'but dat is too funny fer any use. Tell me some mo' 'bout dat noo nigger.'

"So Mars Johnson went on en tol' 'im how he had ter starbe de noo nigger 'fo' he could make 'im take holt er a hoe.

"'Dat wuz de beatinis' notion fer a nigger,' sez Mars Jeems, 'puttin' on airs, des lack he wuz a w'ite man! En I reckon you did n' do nuffin ter 'im?'

"'Oh, no, suh,' sez de oberseah, grinnin' lack a chessy-cat, 'I did n' do nuffin but take de hide off'n 'im.'

"Mars Jeems lafft en lafft, 'tel it 'peared lack he wuz des gwine ter bu'st. '*Tell* me some mo' 'bout dat noo nigger, oh, *tell* me some mo'. Dat noo nigger int'rusts me, he do, en dat is a fac'.'

"Mars Johnson did n' quite un'erstan' w'y Mars Jeems sh'd make sich a great 'miration 'bout de noo nigger, but co'se he want' ter please de gent'eman w'at hi'ed 'im, en so he 'splain' all 'bout how many times he had ter cowhide de noo nigger, en how he made 'im do tasks twicet ez big ez some er de yuther han's, en how he'd chain 'im up in de ba'n at night en feed 'im on co'n-bread en water.

"'Oh! but you is a monst'us good oberseah; you is de bes' oberseah in dis county, Mistah Johnson,' sez Mars Jeems, w'en de oberseah got th'oo wid his tale; 'en dey ain' nebber be'n no nigger-breaker lack you roun' heah befo'. En you desarbes great credit fer sendin' dat nigger 'way befo' you sp'ilt 'im fer de market. Fac', you is sech a monst'us good oberseah, en you is got dis yer plantation in sech fine shape, dat I reckon I doan need you no mo'. You is got dese yer darkies so well train' dat I 'spec' I kin run 'em myse'f fum dis time on. But I does wush you had 'a' hilt on ter dat noo nigger 'tel I got home, fer I 'd 'a' lack ter 'a' seed 'im, I su't'nly should.'

"De oberseah wuz so 'stonish' he did n' ha'dly know w'at ter say, but fin'lly he ax' Mars Jeems ef he would n' gib'im a riccommen' fer ter git ernudder place.

"'No, suh,' sez Mars Jeems, 'somehow er 'nuther I doan lack yo' looks sence I come back dis time, en I'd much ruther you would n' stay roun' heah. Fac', I's feared ef I 'd meet you alone in de woods some time, I mought wanter ha'm you. But layin' dat aside, I be'n lookin' ober dese yer books er yo'n w'at you kep' w'iles I wuz 'way, en fer a yeah er so back, en dere's some figgers w'at ain' des cl'ar ter me. I ain' got no time fer ter talk 'bout 'em now, but I 'spec' befo' I settles wid you fer dis las' mont', you better come up heah ter-morrer, atter I's look' de books en 'counts ober some mo', en den we'll straighten ou' business all up.'

"Mars Jeems 'lowed atterwa'ds dat he wuz des shootin' in de da'k w'en he said dat 'bout de books, but howsomeber, Mars Nick Johnson lef dat naberhood 'twix' de nex' two suns, en nobody roun' dere nebber seed hide ner hair un 'im sence. En all de darkies t'ank de Lawd, en 'lowed it wuz a good riddance er bad rubbage.

"But all dem things I done tol' you ain' nuffin 'side'n de change w'at come ober Mars Jeems fum dat time on. Aun' Peggy's goopher had made a noo man un 'im enti'ely. De nex' day atter he come back, he tol' de han's dey neenter wuk on'y fum sun ter sun, en he cut dey tasks down so dey did n' nobody hab ter stan' ober 'em wid a rawhide er a hick'ry. En he 'lowed ef de niggers want ter hab a dance in de big ba'n any Sad'day night, dey mought hab it. En bimeby, w'en Solomon seed how good Mars Jeems wuz, he ax' 'im ef he would n' please sen' down ter de yuther plantation fer his junesey. Mars Jeems say su't'nly, en gun Solomon a pass en a note ter de oberseah on de yuther plantation, en sont Solomon down ter Robeson County wid a hoss en buggy fer ter fetch his junesey back. Wen de niggers see how fine Mars Jeems gwine treat 'em, dey all tuk ter sweethea'tin' en juneseyin' en singin' en dancin', en eight er ten couples got married, en bimeby eve'ybody 'mence' ter say Mars Jeems McLean got a finer plantation, en slicker-lookin' niggers, en dat he 'uz makin' mo' cotton en co'n, dan any yuther gent'eman in de county. En Mars Jeems's own junesey, Miss Libbie, heared 'bout de noo gwines-on on Mars Jeems's plantation, en she change' her min' 'bout Mars Jeems en tuk 'im back ag'in, en 'fo' long dey had a fine weddin', en all de darkies had a big feas', en dey wuz fiddlin' en dancin' en funnin' en frolic'in' fum sundown 'tel mawnin'."

"And they all lived happy ever after," I said, as the old man reached a full stop.

"Yas, suh," he said, interpreting my remarks as a question, "dey did. Solomon useter say," he added, "dat Aun' Peggy's goopher had turnt Mars Jeems ter a nigger, en dat dat noo ban' wuz Mars Jeems hisse'f. But co'se Solomon did n' das' ter let on 'bout w'at he 'spicioned, en ole Aun' Peggy would 'a' 'nied it ef she had be'n ax', fer she 'd 'a' got in trouble sho', ef it 'uz knowed she 'd be'n cunj'in' de w'ite folks.

"Dis yer tale goes ter show," concluded Julius sententiously, as the man came up and announced that the spring was ready for us to get water, "dat w'ite folks w'at is so ha'd en stric', en doan make no 'lowance fer po' ign'ant niggers w'at ain' had no chanst ter l'arn, is li'ble ter hab bad dreams, ter say de leas', en dat dem w'at is kin' en good ter po' people is sho' ter prosper en git 'long in de worl'."

"That is a very strange story, Uncle Julius," observed my wife, smiling, "and Solomon's explanation is quite improbable."

"Yes, Julius," said I, "that was powerful goopher. I am glad, too, that you told us the moral of the story; it might have escaped us otherwise. By the way, did you make that up all by yourself?"

The old man's face assumed an injured look, expressive more of sorrow than of anger, and shaking his head he replied:—

"No, suh, I heared dat tale befo' you er Mis' Annie dere wuz bawn, suh. My mammy tol' me dat tale w'en I wa'n't mo' d'n knee-high ter a hopper-grass."

I drove to town next morning, on some business, and did not return until noon; and after dinner I had to visit a neighbor, and did not get back until supper-time. I was smoking a cigar on the back piazza in the early evening, when I saw a familiar figure carrying a bucket of water to the barn. I called my wife.

"My dear," I said severely, "what is that rascal doing here? I thought I discharged him yesterday for good and all."

"Oh, yes," she answered, "I forgot to tell you. He was hanging round the place all the morning, and looking so down in the mouth, that I told him that if he would try to do better, we would give him one more chance. He seems so grateful, and so really in earnest in his promises of amendment, that I'm sure you'll not regret taking him back."

I was seriously enough annoyed to let my cigar go out. I did not share my wife's rose-colored hopes in regard to Tom; but as I did not wish the servants to think there was any conflict of authority in the household, I let the boy stay.

# The Conjurer's Revenge

S unday was sometimes a rather dull day at our place. In the morning, when the weather was pleasant, my wife and I would drive to town, a distance of about five miles, to attend the church of our choice. The afternoons we spent at home, for the most part, occupying ourselves with the newspapers and magazines, and the contents of a fairly good library. We had a piano in the house, on which my wife played with skill and feeling. I possessed a passable baritone voice, and could accompany myself indifferently well when my wife was not by to assist me. When these resources failed us, we were apt to find it a little dull.

One Sunday afternoon in early spring,—the balmy spring of North Carolina, when the air is in that ideal balance between heat and cold where one wishes it could always remain,—my wife and I were seated on the front piazza, she wearily but conscientiously ploughing through a missionary report, while I followed the impossible career of the blonde heroine of a rudimentary novel. I had thrown the book aside in disgust, when I saw Julius coming through the yard, under the spreading elms, which were already in full leaf. He wore his Sunday clothes, and advanced with a dignity of movement quite different from his week-day slouch.

"Have a seat, Julius," I said, pointing to an empty rocking-chair.

"No, thanky, boss, I'll des set here on de top step."

"Oh, no, Uncle Julius," exclaimed Annie, "take this chair. You will find it much more comfortable."

The old man grinned in appreciation of her solicitude, and seated himself somewhat awkwardly.

"Julius," I remarked, "I am thinking of setting out scuppernong vines on that sand-hill where the three persimmon-trees are; and while I'm working there, I think I'll plant watermelons between the vines, and get a little something to pay for my first year's work. The new railroad will be finished by the middle of summer, and I can ship the melons North, and get a good price for them."

"Ef you er gwine ter hab any mo' ploughin' ter do," replied Julius, "I 'spec' you'll ha' ter buy ernudder creetur, 'ca'se hit's much ez dem hosses kin do ter 'ten' ter de wuk dey got now."

"Yes, I had thought of that. I think I'll get a mule; a mule can do more work, and doesn't require as much attention as a horse."

"I would n' 'vise you ter buy no mule," remarked Julius, with a shake of his head.

"Why not?"

"Well, you may 'low hit's all foolis'ness, but ef I wuz in yo' place, I would n' buy no mule."

"But that isn't a reason; what objection have you to a mule?"

"Fac' is," continued the old man, in a serious tone, "I doan lack ter dribe a mule. I 's alluz afeared I mought be imposin' on some human creetur; eve'y time I cuts a mule wid a hick'ry, 'pears ter me mos' lackly I's cuttin' some er my own relations, er somebody e'se w'at can't he'p deyse'ves."

"What put such an absurd idea into your head?" I asked.

My question was followed by a short silence, during which Julius seemed engaged in a mental struggle.

"I dunno ez hit's wuf w'ile ter tell you dis," he said, at length. "I doan ha'dly 'spec' fer you ter b'lieve it. Does you 'member dat club-footed man w'at hilt de hoss fer you de yuther day w'en you was gittin' out'n de rockaway down ter Mars Archie McMillan's sto'?"

"Yes, I believe I do remember seeing a club-footed man there."

"Did you eber see a club-footed nigger befo' er sence?"

"No, I can't remember that I ever saw a club-footed colored man," I replied, after a moment's reflection.

"You en Mis' Annie would n' wanter b'lieve me, ef I wuz ter 'low dat dat man was oncet a mule?"

"No," I replied, "I don't think it very likely that you could make us believe it."

"Why, Uncle Julius!" said Annie severely, "what ridiculous nonsense!"

This reception of the old man's statement reduced him to silence, and it required some diplomacy on my part to induce him to vouchsafe an explanation. The prospect of a long, dull afternoon was not alluring, and I was glad to have the monotony of Sabbath quiet relieved by a plantation legend.

"W'en I wuz a young man," began Julius, when I had finally prevailed upon him to tell us the story, "dat club-footed nigger—his name is Primus—use' ter b'long ter ole Mars Jim McGee ober on de Lumbe'ton plank-road. I use' ter go ober dere ter see a 'oman w'at libbed on de plantation; dat 's how I come ter know all erbout it. Dis yer Primus wuz de livelies' han' on de place, alluz a-dancin', en drinkin', en runnin' roun', en singin', en pickin' de banjo; 'cep'n' once in a w'ile, w'en he 'd 'low he

CHARLES W. CHESNUTT

wa'n't treated right 'bout sump'n ernudder, he'd git so sulky en stubborn dat de w'ite folks could n' ha'dly do nuffin wid 'im.

"It wuz 'gin' de rules fer any er de han's ter go 'way fum de plantation at night; but Primus did n' min' de rules, en went w'en he felt lack it; en de w'ite folks purten' lack dey did n' know it, fer Primus was dange'ous w'en he got in dem stubborn spells, en dey 'd ruther not fool wid 'im.

"One night in de spring er de year, Primus slip' off fum de plantation, en went down on de Wim'l'ton Road ter a dance gun by some er de free niggers down dere. Dey wuz a fiddle, en a banjo, en a jug gwine roun' on de outside, en Primus sung en dance' 'tel 'long 'bout two o'clock in de mawnin', w'en he start' fer home. Ez he come erlong back, he tuk a nigh-cut 'cross de cottonfiel's en 'long by de aidge er de Min'al Spring Swamp, so ez ter git shet er de patteroles w'at rid up en down de big road fer ter keep de darkies fum runnin' roun' nights. Primus was sa'nt'rin' 'long, studyin' 'bout de good time he 'd had wid de gals, w'en, ez he wuz gwine by a fence co'nder, w'at sh'd he heah but sump'n grunt. He stopped a minute ter listen, en he heared sump'n grunt ag'in. Den he went ober ter de fence whar he heard de fuss, en dere, layin' in de fence co'nder, on a pile er pine straw, he seed a fine, fat shote.

"Primus look' ha'd at de shote, en den sta'ted home. But somehow er 'nudder he could n' git away fum dat shote; w'en he tuk one step for'ards wid one foot, de yuther foot 'peared ter take two steps back'ards, en so he kep' nachly gittin' closeter en closeter ter de shote. It was de beatin'es' thing! De shote des 'peared ter cha'm Primus, en fus' thing you know Primus foun' hisse'f 'way up de road wid de shote on his back.

"Ef Primus had 'a' knowed whose shote dat wuz, he 'd 'a' manage' ter git pas' it somehow er 'nudder. Ez it happen', de shote b'long ter a cunjuh man w'at libbed down in de free-nigger sett'ement. Co'se de cunjuh man did n' hab ter wuk his roots but a little w'ile 'fo' he foun' out who tuk his shote, en den de trouble begun. One mawnin', a day er so later, en befo' he got de shote eat up, Primus did n' go ter wuk w'en de hawn blow, en w'en de oberseah wen' ter look fer him, dey wa' no trace er Primus ter be 'skivered nowhar. W'en he did n' come back in a day er so mo', eve'ybody on de plantation 'lowed he had runned erway. His marster a'vertise' him in de papers, en offered a big reward fer 'im. De nigger-ketchers fotch out dey dogs, en track' 'im down ter de aidge er de swamp, en den de scent gun out; en dat was de las' anybody seed er Primus fer a long, long time.

"Two er th'ee weeks atter Primus disappear', his marster went ter town one Sad'day. Mars Jim was stan'in' in front er Sandy Campbell's bar-room, up by de ole wagon-ya'd, w'en a po' w'ite man fum down on de Wim'l'ton Road come up ter 'im en ax' 'im, kinder keerless lack, ef he did n' wanter buy a mule.

"'I dunno,' says Mars Jim; 'it 'pen's on de mule, en on de price. Whar is de mule?'

"'Des 'roun' heah back er ole Tom McAllister's sto',' says de po' w'ite man.

"'I reckon I'll hab a look at de mule,' says Mars Jim, 'en ef he suit me, I dunno but w'at I mought buy 'im.'

"So de po' w'ite man tuk Mars Jim 'roun' back er de sto', en dere stood a monst'us fine mule. W'en de mule see Mars Jim, he gun a whinny, des lack he knowed him befo'. Mars Jim look' at de mule, en de mule 'peared ter be soun' en strong. Mars Jim 'lowed dey 'peared ter be sump'n fermilyus 'bout de mule's face, 'spesh'ly his eyes; but he had n' los' naer mule, en did n' hab no recommemb'ance er habin' seed de mule befo'. He ax' de po' buckrah whar he got de mule, en de po' buckrah say his brer raise' de mule down on Rockfish Creek. Mars Jim was a little s'picious er seein' a po' w'ite man wid sech a fine creetur, but he fin'lly 'greed ter gib de man fifty dollars fer de mule,—'bout ha'f w'at a good mule was wuf dem days.

"He tied de mule behin' de buggy w'en he went home, en put 'im ter ploughin' cotton de nex' day. De mule done mighty well fer th'ee er fo' days, en den de niggers 'mence' ter notice some quare things erbout him. Dey wuz a medder on de plantation whar dey use' ter put de hosses en mules ter pastur'. Hit was fence' off fum de cornfiel' on one side, but on de yuther side'n de pastur' was a terbacker-patch w'at wa'n't fence' off, 'ca'se de beastisses doan none un 'em eat terbacker. Dey doan know w'at 's good! Terbacker is lack religion, de good Lawd made it fer people, en dey ain' no yuther creetur w'at kin 'preciate it. De darkies notice' dat de fus' thing de new mule done, w'en he was turnt inter de pastur', wuz ter make fer de terbacker-patch. Co'se dey didn' think nuffin un it, but nex' mawnin', w'en dey went ter ketch 'im, dey 'skivered dat he had eat up two whole rows er terbacker plants. Atter dat dey had ter put a halter on 'im, en tie 'im ter a stake, er e'se dey would n' 'a' been naer leaf er terbacker lef' in de patch.

"Ernudder day one er de han's, name' 'Dolphus, hitch' de mule up, en dribe up here ter dis yer vimya'd,—dat wuz w'en ole Mars Dugal' own' dis place. Mars Dugal' had kilt a yearlin', en de naber w'ite folks all sont ober fer ter git some fraish beef, en Mars Jim had sont 'Dolphus fer some too. Dey wuz a winepress in de ya'd whar 'Dolphus lef' de mule a-stan'in', en right in front er de press dey wuz a tub er grape-juice, des pressed out, en a little ter one side a bairl erbout half full er wine w'at had be'n stan'in' two er th'ee days, en had begun ter git sorter sha'p ter de tas'e. Dey wuz a couple er bo'ds on top er dis yer bairl, wid a rock laid on 'em ter hol' 'em down. Ez I wuz a-sayin', 'Dolphus lef' de mule stan'in' in de ya'd, en went inter de smoke-house fer ter git de beef. Bimeby, w'en he come out, he seed de mule a-stagg'rin' 'bout de ya'd; en 'fo' 'Dolphus could git dere ter fin' out w'at wuz de matter, de mule fell right ober on his side, en laid dere des' lack he was dead.

"All de niggers 'bout de house run out dere fer ter see w'at wuz de matter. Some say de mule had de colic; some say one thing en some ernudder; 'tel bimeby one er de han's seed de top wuz off'n de bairl, en run en looked in.

"'Fo' de Lawd!' he say, 'dat mule drunk! he be'n drinkin' de wine.' En sho' 'nuff, de mule had pas' right by de tub er fraish grape-juice en push' de kiver off'n de bairl, en drunk two er th'ee gallon er de wine w'at had been stan'in' long ernough fer ter begin ter git sha'p.

"De darkies all made a great 'miration 'bout de mule gittin' drunk. Dey never had n' seed nuffin lack it in dey bawn days. Dey po'd water ober de mule, en tried ter sober 'im up; but it wa'n't no use, en 'Dolphus had ter take de beef home on his back, en leabe de mule dere, 'tel he slep' off 'is spree.

"I doan 'member whe'r I tol' you er no, but w'en Primus disappear' fum de plantation, he lef' a wife behin' 'im,—a monst'us good-lookin' yaller gal, name' Sally. W'en Primus had be'n gone a mont' er so, Sally 'mence' fer ter git lonesome, en tuk up wid ernudder young man name' Dan, w'at b'long' on de same plantation. One day dis yer Dan tuk de noo mule out in de cotton-fiel' fer ter plough, en w'en dey wuz gwine 'long de tu'n-row, who sh'd he meet but dis yer Sally. Dan look' 'roun' en he did n' see de oberseah nowhar, so he stop' a minute fer ter run on wid Sally.

"'Hoddy, honey,' sezee. 'How you feelin' dis mawnin'?'

"'Fus' rate,' 'spon' Sally.

"Dey wuz lookin' at one ernudder, en dey did n' naer one un 'em pay no 'tention ter de mule, who had turnt 'is head 'roun' en wuz lookin' at Sally ez ha'd ez he could, en stretchin' 'is neck en raisin' 'is years, en whinnyin' kinder sof' ter hisse'f.

"'Yas, honey,' 'lows Dan, 'en you gwine ter feel fus' rate long ez you sticks ter me. Fer I's a better man dan dat low-down runaway nigger Primus dat you be'n wastin' yo' time wid.'

"Dan had let go de plough-handle, en had put his arm 'roun' Sally, en wuz des gwine ter kiss her, w'en sump'n ketch' 'im by de scruff er de neck en flung 'im 'way ober in de cotton-patch. W'en he pick' 'isse'f up, Sally had gone kitin' down de tu'n-row, en de mule wuz stan'in' dere lookin' ez ca'm en peaceful ez a Sunday mawnin'.

"Fus' Dan had 'lowed it wuz de oberseah w'at had cotch' 'im wastin' 'is time. But dey wa'n't no oberseah in sight, so he 'cluded it must 'a' be'n de mule. So he pitch' inter de mule en lammed 'im ez ha'd ez he could. De mule tuk it all, en 'peared ter be ez 'umble ez a mule could be; but w'en dey wuz makin' de turn at de een' er de row, one er de plough-lines got under de mule's hin' leg. Dan retch' down ter git de line out, sorter keerless like, w'en de mule haul' off en kick him clean ober de fence inter a brier-patch on de yuther side.

"Dan wuz mighty so' fum 'is woun's en scratches, en wuz laid up fer two er th'ee days. One night de noo mule got out'n de pastur', en went down to de quarters. Dan wuz layin' dere on his pallet, w'en he heard sump'n bangin' erway at de side er his cabin. He raise' up on one shoulder en look' roun', w'en w'at should he see but de noo mule's head stickin' in de winder, wid his lips drawed back over his toofs, grinnin' en snappin' at Dan des' lack he wanter eat 'im up. Den de mule went roun' ter de do', en kick' erway lack he wanter break de do' down, 'tel bimeby somebody come 'long en driv him back ter de pastur'. W'en Sally come in a little later fum de big house, whar she 'd be'n waitin' on de w'ite folks, she foun' po' Dan nigh 'bout dead, he wuz so skeered. She 'lowed Dan had had de nightmare; but w'en dey look' at de do', dey seed de marks er de mule's huffs, so dey could n' be no mistake 'bout w'at had happen'.

"Co'se de niggers tol' dey marster 'bout de mule's gwines-on. Fust he did n' pay no 'tention ter it, but atter a w'ile he tol' 'em ef dey did n' stop dey foolis'ness, he gwine tie some un 'em up. So atter dat dey did n' say nuffin mo' ter dey marster, but dey kep' on noticin' de mule's quare ways des de same.

"'Long 'bout de middle er de summer dey wuz a big camp-meetin' broke out down on de Wim'l'ton Road, en nigh 'bout all de po' w'ite folks en free niggers in de settlement got 'ligion, en lo en behol'! 'mongs' 'em wuz de cunjuh man w'at own' de shote w'at cha'med Primus.

"Dis cunjuh man wuz a Guinea nigger, en befo' he wuz sot free had use' ter b'long ter a gent'eman down in Sampson County. De cunjuh man say his daddy wuz a king, er a guv'ner, er some sorter w'at-you-may-call-'em 'way ober yander in Affiky whar de niggers come fum, befo' he was stoled erway en sol' ter de spekilaters. De cunjuh man had he'ped his marster out'n some trouble ernudder wid his goopher, en his marster had sot him free, en bought him a trac' er land down on de Wim'l'ton Road. He purten' ter be a cow-doctor, but eve'ybody knowed w'at he r'al'y wuz.

"De cunjuh man had n' mo' d'n come th'oo good, befo' he wuz tuk sick wid a col' w'at he kotch kneelin' on de groun' so long at de mou'ners' bench. He kep' gittin' wusser en wusser, en bimeby de rheumatiz tuk holt er 'im, en drawed him all up, 'tel one day he sont word up ter Mars Jim McGee's plantation, en ax' Pete, de nigger w'at tuk keer er de mules, fer ter come down dere dat night en fetch dat mule w'at his marster had bought fum de po' w'ite man dyoin' er de summer.

"Pete did n' know w'at de cunjuh man wuz dribin' at, but he did n' daster stay way; en so dat night, w'en he 'd done eat his bacon en his hoe-cake, en drunk his 'lasses-en-water, he put a bridle on de mule, en rid 'im down ter de cunjuh man's cabin. W'en he got ter de do', he lit en hitch' de mule, en den knock' at de do'. He felt mighty jubous 'bout gwine in, but he was bleedst ter do it; he knowed he could n' he'p 'isse'f.

"'Pull de string,' sez a weak voice, en w'en Pete lif de latch en went in, de cunjuh man was layin' on de bed, lookin' pale en weak, lack he did n' hab much longer fer ter lib.

"'Is you fotch' de mule?' sezee.

"Pete say yas, en de cunjuh man kep' on.

"'Brer Pete,' sezee, 'I's be'n a monst'us sinner man, en I's done a power er wickedness endyoin' er my days; but de good Lawd is wash' my sins erway, en I feels now dat I's boun' fer de kingdom. En I feels, too, dat I ain' gwine ter git up fum dis bed no mo' in dis worl', en I wants ter ondo some er de harm I done. En dat's de reason, Brer Pete, I sont fer you ter fetch dat mule down here. You 'member dat shote I was up ter yo' plantation inquirin' 'bout las' June?'

"'Yas,' says Brer Pete, 'I'member yo' axin' 'bout a shote you had los'.'

"'I dunno whe'r you eber l'arnt it er no,' says de cunjuh man, 'but I done knowed yo' marster's Primus had tuk de shote, en I wuz boun' ter git eben wid 'im. So one night I cotch' 'im down by de swamp on his way ter a candy-pullin', en I th'owed a goopher mixtry on 'im, en turnt 'im ter a mule, en got a po' w'ite man ter sell de mule, en we 'vided de money. But I doan want ter die 'tel I turn Brer Primus back ag'in.'

"Den de cunjuh man ax' Pete ter take down one er two go'ds off'n a she'f in de corner, en one er two bottles wid some kin' er mixtry in 'em, en set 'em on a stool by de bed; en den he ax' 'im ter fetch de mule in.

"W'en de mule come in de do', he gin a snort, en started fer de bed, des lack he was gwine ter jump on it.

"'Hol' on dere, Brer Primus!' de cunjuh man hollered. 'I's monst'us weak, en ef you 'mence on me, you won't nebber hab no chance fer ter git turn' back no mo'.'

"De mule seed de sense er dat, en stood still. Den de cunjuh man tuk de go'ds en bottles, en 'mence' ter wuk de roots en yarbs, en de mule 'mence' ter turn back ter a man,—fust his years, den de res' er his head, den his shoulders en arms. All de time de cunjuh man kep' on wukkin' his roots; en Pete en Primus could see he wuz gittin' weaker en weaker all de time.

"'Brer Pete,' sezee, bimeby, 'gimme a drink er dem bitters out'n dat green bottle on de she'f yander. I's gwine fas', en it'll gimme strenk fer ter finish dis wuk.'

"Brer Pete look' up on de mantelpiece, en he seed a bottle in de corner. It was so da'k in de cabin he could n' tell whe'r it wuz a green bottle er no. But he hilt de bottle ter de cunjuh man's mouf, en he tuk a big mouff'l. He had n' mo' d'n swallowed it befo' he 'mence' ter holler.

"'You gimme de wrong bottle, Brer Pete; dis yer bottle 's got pizen in it, en I's done fer dis time, sho'. Hol' me up, fer de Lawd's sake! 'tel I git th'oo turnin' Brer Primus back.'

"So Pete hilt him up, en he kep' on wukkin' de roots, 'tel he got de goopher all tuk off'n Brer Primus 'cep'n' one foot. He had n' got dis foot mo' d'n half turnt back befo' his strenk gun out enti'ely, en he drap' de roots en fell back on de bed.

"'I can't do no mo' fer you, Brer Primus,' sezee, 'but I hopes you will fergib me fer w'at harm I done you. I knows de good Lawd done fergib me, en I hope ter meet you bofe in glory. I sees de good angels waitin' fer me up yander, wid a long w'ite robe en a starry crown, en I'm on my way ter jine 'em.' En so de cunjuh man died, en Pete en Primus went back ter de plantation.

"De darkies all made a great 'miration w'en Primus come back. Mars Jim let on lack he did n' b'lieve de tale de two niggers tol'; he sez Primus had runned erway, en stay' 'tel he got ti'ed er de swamps, en den come back on him ter be fed. He tried ter 'count fer de shape er Primus' foot by sayin' Primus got his foot smash', er snake-bit, er sump'n, w'iles he wuz erway, en den stayed out in de woods whar he could n' git it kyoed up straight, 'stidder comin' long home whar a doctor could 'a' 'tended ter it. But de niggers all notice' dey marster did n' tie Primus up, ner take on much 'ca'se de mule wuz gone. So dey 'lowed dey marster must 'a' had his s'picions 'bout dat cunjuh man."

My wife had listened to Julius's recital with only a mild interest. When the old man had finished it she remarked:—

"That story does not appeal to me, Uncle Julius, and is not up to your usual mark. It isn't pathetic, it has no moral that I can discover, and I can't see why you should tell it. In fact, it seems to me like nonsense."

The old man looked puzzled as well as pained. He had not pleased the lady, and he did not seem to understand why.

"I'm sorry, ma'm," he said reproachfully, "ef you doan lack dat tale. I can't make out w'at you means by some er dem wo'ds you uses, but I'm tellin' nuffin but de truf. Co'se I did n' see de cunjuh man tu'n 'im back, fer I wuz n' dere; but I be'n hearin' de tale fer twenty-five yeahs, en I ain' got no 'casion fer ter 'spute it. Dey 's so many things a body knows is lies, dat dey ain' no use gwine roun' findin' fault wid tales dat mought des ez well be so ez not. F' instance, dey 's a young nigger gwine ter school in town, en he come out heah de yuther day en 'lowed dat de sun stood still en de yeath turnt roun' eve'y day on a kinder axletree. I tol' dat young nigger ef he didn' take hisse'f 'way wid dem lies, I 'd take a buggy-trace ter 'im; fer I sees de yeath stan'in' still all de time, en I sees de sun gwine roun' it, en ef a man can't b'lieve w'at 'e sees, I can't see no use in libbin'—mought's well die en be whar we can't see nuffin. En ernudder thing w'at proves de tale 'bout dis ole Primus is de way he goes on ef anybody ax' him how he come by dat club-foot. I axed 'im one day, mighty perlite en civil, en he call' me a' ole fool, en got so mad he ain' spoke ter me sence. Hit's monst'us quare. But dis is a quare worl', anyway yer kin fix it," concluded the old man, with a weary sigh.

"Ef you makes up yo' min' not ter buy dat mule, suh," he added, as he rose to go, "I knows a man w'at 's got a good hoss he wants ter sell,—leas'ways dat's w'at I heared. I'm gwine ter pra'rmeetin' ter-night, en I'm gwine right by de man's house, en ef you 'd lack ter look at de hoss, I'll ax 'im ter fetch him roun'."

"Oh, yes," I said, "you can ask him to stop in, if he is passing. There will be no harm in looking at the horse, though I rather think I shall buy a mule."

Early next morning the man brought the horse up to the vineyard. At that time I was not a very good judge of horseflesh. The horse appeared sound and gentle, and, as the owner assured me, had no bad habits. The man wanted a large price for the horse, but finally agreed to accept a much smaller sum, upon payment of which I became possessed of a very fine-looking animal. But alas for the deceitfulness of appearances! I soon ascertained that the horse was blind in one eye, and that the sight of the other was very defective; and not a month elapsed before my purchase developed most of the diseases that horse-flesh is heir to, and a more worthless, broken-winded, spavined quadruped never disgraced the noble name of horse. After worrying through two or three months of life, he expired one night in a fit of the colic. I replaced him with a mule, and Julius henceforth had to take his chances of driving some metamorphosed unfortunate.

Circumstances that afterwards came to my knowledge created in my mind a strong suspicion that Julius may have played a more than unconscious part in this transaction. Among other significant facts was his appearance, the Sunday following the purchase of the horse, in a new suit of store clothes, which I had seen displayed in the window of Mr. Solomon Cohen's store on my last visit to town, and had remarked on account of their striking originality of cut and pattern. As I had not recently paid Julius any money, and as he had no property to mortgage, I was driven to conjecture to account for his possession of the means to buy the clothes. Of course I would not charge him with duplicity unless I could prove it, at least to a moral certainty, but for a long time afterwards I took his advice only in small doses and with great discrimination.

CHARLES W. CHESNUTT

# Sis' Becky's Pickaninny

W e had not lived in North Carolina very long before I was able to note a marked improvement in my wife's health. The ozone-laden air of the surrounding piney woods, the mild and equable climate, the peaceful leisure of country life, had brought about in hopeful measure the cure we had anticipated. Toward the end of our second year, however, her ailment took an unexpected turn for the worse. She became the victim of a settled melancholy, attended with vague forebodings of impending misfortune.

"You must keep up her spirits," said our physician, the best in the neighboring town. "This melancholy lowers her tone too much, tends to lessen her strength, and, if it continue too long, may be fraught with grave consequences."

I tried various expedients to cheer her up. I read novels to her. I had the hands on the place come up in the evening and serenade her with plantation songs. Friends came in sometimes and talked, and frequent letters from the North kept her in touch with her former home. But nothing seemed to rouse her from the depression into which she had fallen.

One pleasant afternoon in spring, I placed an armchair in a shaded portion of the front piazza, and filling it with pillows led my wife out of the house and seated her where she would have the pleasantest view of a somewhat monotonous scenery. She was scarcely placed when old Julius came through the yard, and, taking off his tattered straw hat, inquired, somewhat anxiously:—

"How is you feelin' dis afternoon, ma'm?"

"She is not very cheerful, Julius," I said. My wife was apparently without energy enough to speak for herself.

The old man did not seem inclined to go away, so I asked him to sit down. I had noticed, as he came up, that he held some small object in his hand. When he had taken his seat on the top step, he kept fingering this object,—what it was I could not quite make out.

"What is that you have there, Julius?" I asked, with mild curiosity.

"Dis is my rabbit foot, suh."

This was at a time before this curious superstition had attained its present jocular popularity among white people, and while I had heard of it before, it had not yet outgrown the charm of novelty.

"What do you do with it?"

"I kyars it wid me fer luck, suh."

"Julius," I observed, half to him and half to my wife, "your people will never rise in the world until they throw off these childish superstitions and learn to live by the light of reason and common sense. How absurd to imagine that the fore-foot of a poor dead rabbit, with which he timorously felt his way along through a life surrounded by snares and pitfalls, beset by enemies on every hand, can promote happiness or success, or ward off failure or misfortune!"

"It is ridiculous," assented my wife, with faint interest.

"Dat's w'at I tells dese niggers roun' heah," said Julius. "De fo'-foot ain' got no power. It has ter be de hin'-foot, suh,—de lef hin'-foot er a grabe-ya'd rabbit, killt by a cross-eyed nigger on a da'k night in de full er de moon."

"They must be very rare and valuable," I said.

"Dey is kinder ska'ce, suh, en dey ain' no 'mount er money could buy mine, suh. I mought len' it ter anybody I sot sto' by, but I would n' sell it, no indeed, suh, I would n'."

"How do you know it brings good luck?" I asked.

"'Ca'se I ain' had no bad luck sence I had it, suh, en I's had dis rabbit foot fer fo'ty yeahs. I had a good marster befo' de wah, en I wa'n't sol' erway, en I wuz sot free; en dat 'uz all good luck."

"But that doesn't prove anything," I rejoined. "Many other people have gone through a similar experience, and probably more than one of them had no rabbit's foot."

"Law, suh! you doan hafter prove 'bout de rabbit foot! Eve'ybody knows dat; leas'ways eve'ybody roun' heah knows it. But ef it has ter be prove' ter folks w'at wa'n't bawn en raise' in dis naberhood, dey is a' easy way ter prove it. Is I eber tol' you de tale er Sis' Becky en her pickaninny?"

"No," I said, "let us hear it." I thought perhaps the story might interest my wife as much or more than the novel I had meant to read from.

"Dis yer Becky," Julius began, "useter b'long ter ole Kunnel Pen'leton, who owned a plantation down on de Wim'l'ton Road, 'bout ten miles fum heah, des befo' you gits ter Black Swamp. Dis yer Becky wuz a fiel'-han', en a monst'us good 'un. She had a husban' oncet, a nigger w'at b'longed on de nex' plantation, but de man w'at owned her husban' died, en his lan' en his niggers had ter be sol' fer ter pay his debts. Kunnel Pen'leton 'lowed he'd 'a' bought dis nigger, but he had be'n bettin' on hoss races, en did n' hab no money, en so Becky's husban' wuz sol' erway ter Fuhginny.

"Co'se Becky went on some 'bout losin' her man, but she could n' he'p herse'f; en 'sides dat, she had her pickaninny fer ter comfo't her. Dis yer little Mose wuz de cutes', blackes', shiny-eyedes' little nigger you eber laid eyes on, en he wuz ez fon' er his mammy ez his mammy wuz er him. Co'se Becky had ter wuk en did n' hab much time ter was'e wid her baby. Ole Aun' Nancy, de plantation nuss down at de qua'ters, useter take keer er little Mose in de daytime, en atter de niggers come in fum de cotton-fiel' Becky 'ud git her chile en kiss 'im en nuss 'im, en keep 'im 'tel mawnin'; en on Sundays she 'd hab 'im in her cabin wid her all day long.

"Sis' Becky had got sorter useter gittin' 'long widout her husban', w'en one day Kunnel Pen'leton went ter de races. Co'se w'en he went ter de races, he tuk his hosses, en co'se he bet on 'is own hosses, en co'se he los' his money; fer Kunnel Pen'leton did n' nebber hab no luck wid his hosses, ef he did keep hisse'f po' projeckin' wid 'em. But dis time dey wuz a hoss name' Lightnin' Bug, w'at b'longed ter ernudder man, en dis hoss won de sweep-stakes; en Kunnel Pen'leton tuk a lackin' ter dat hoss, en ax' his owner w'at he wuz willin' ter take fer 'im.

"'I'll take a thousan' dollahs fer dat hoss,' sez dis yer man, who had a big plantation down to'ds Wim'l'ton, whar he raise' hosses fer ter race en ter sell.

"Well, Kunnel Pen'leton scratch' 'is head, en wonder whar he wuz gwine ter raise a thousan' dollahs; en he did n' see des how he could do it, fer he owed ez much ez he could borry a'ready on de skyo'ity he could gib. But he wuz des boun' ter hab dat hoss, so sezee:—

"'I'll gib you my note fer' 'leven hund'ed dollahs fer dat hoss.'

"De yuther man shuck 'is head, en sezee:—

"'Yo' note, suh, is better 'n gol', I doan doubt; but I is made it a rule in my bizness not ter take no notes fum nobody. Howsomeber, suh, ef you is kinder sho't er fun's, mos' lackly we kin make some kin' er bahg'in. En w'iles we is talkin', I mought 's well say dat I needs ernudder good nigger down on my place. Ef you is got a good one ter spar', I mought trade wid you.'

"Now, Kunnel Pen'leton did n' r'ally hab no niggers fer ter spar', but he 'lowed ter hisse'f he wuz des bleedzd ter hab dat hoss, en so he sez, sezee:—

"'Well, I doan lack ter, but I reckon I'll haf ter. You come out ter my plantation ter-morrer en look ober my niggers, en pick out de one you wants.'

"So sho' 'nuff nex' day dis yer man come out ter Kunnel Pen'leton's place en rid roun' de plantation en glanshed at de niggers, en who sh'd he pick out fum 'em all but Sis' Becky.

"'I needs a noo nigger 'oman down ter my place,' sezee, 'fer ter cook en wash, en so on; en dat young 'oman'll des fill de bill. You gimme her, en you kin hab Lightnin' Bug.'"

"Now, Kunnel Pen'leton did n' lack ter trade Sis' Becky, 'ca'se she wuz nigh 'bout de bes' fiel'-han' he had; en 'sides, Mars Kunnel did n' keer ter take de mammies 'way fum dey chillun w'iles de chillun wuz little. But dis man say he want Becky, er e'se Kunnel Pen'leton could n' hab de race hoss.

"'Well,' sez de kunnel, 'you kin hab de 'oman. But I doan lack ter sen' her 'way fum her baby. W'at'll you gimme fer dat nigger baby?'

"'I doan want de baby,' sez de yuther man. 'I ain' got no use fer de baby.'

"'I tell yer w'at I'll do,' 'lows Kunnel Pen'leton, 'I'll th'ow dat pickaninny in fer good measure.'

"But de yuther man shuck his head. 'No,' sezee, 'I's much erbleedzd, but I doan raise niggers; I raises hosses, en I doan wanter be both'rin' wid no nigger babies. Nemmine de baby. I'll keep dat 'oman so busy she 'll fergit de baby; fer niggers is made ter wuk, en dey ain' got no time fer no sich foolis'ness ez babies.'

"Kunnel Pen'leton did n' wanter hu't Becky's feelin's,—fer Kunnel Pen'leton wuz a kin'-hea'ted man, en nebber lack' ter make no trouble fer nobody,—en so he tol' Becky he wuz gwine sen' her down ter Robeson County fer a day er so, ter he'p out his son-in-law in his wuk; en bein' ez dis yuther man wuz gwine dat way, he had ax' 'im ter take her 'long in his buggy.

"'Kin I kyar little Mose wid me, marster?' ax' Sis' Becky.

"'N-o,' sez de kunnel, ez ef he wuz studyin' whuther ter let her take 'im er no;' I reckon you better let Aun' Nancy look atter yo' baby fer de day er two you'll be gone, en she'll see dat he gits ernuff ter eat 'tel you gits back.'

"So Sis' Becky hug' en kiss' little Mose, en tol' 'im ter be a good little pickaninny, en take keer er hisse'f, en not fergit his mammy w'iles she wuz gone. En little Mose put his arms roun' his mammy en lafft en crowed des lack it wuz monst'us fine fun fer his mammy ter go 'way en leabe 'im.

"Well, dis yer hoss trader sta'ted out wid Becky, en bimeby, atter dey'd gone down de Lumbe'ton Road fer a few miles er so, dis man tu'nt roun' in a diffe'nt d'rection, en kep' goin' dat erway, 'tel bimeby Sis' Becky up 'n ax''im ef he wuz gwine' ter Robeson County by a noo road.

"'No, nigger,' sezee, 'I ain' gwine ter Robeson County at all. I's gwine ter Bladen County, whar my plantation is, en whar I raises all my hosses.'

"'But how is I gwine ter git ter Mis' Laura's plantation down in Robeson County?' sez Becky, wid her hea't in her mouf, fer she 'mence' ter git skeered all er a sudden.

"'You ain' gwine ter git dere at all,' sez de man. 'You b'longs ter me now, fer I done traded my bes' race hoss fer you, wid yo' ole marster. Ef you is a good gal, I'll treat you right, en ef you doan behabe yo'se'f,—w'y, w'at e'se happens'll be yo' own fault.'

"Co'se Sis' Becky cried en went on 'bout her pickaninny, but co'se it did n' do no good, en bimeby dey got down ter dis yer man's place, en he put Sis' Becky ter wuk, en fergot all 'bout her habin' a pickaninny.

"Meanw'iles, w'en ebenin' come, de day Sis' Becky wuz tuk 'way, little Mose mence' ter git res'less, en bimeby, w'en his mammy did n' come, he sta'ted ter cry fer 'er. Aun' Nancy fed 'im en rocked 'im en rocked 'im, en fin'lly he des cried en cried 'tel he cried hisse'f ter sleep.

"De nex' day he did n' 'pear ter be as peart ez yushal, en w'en night come he fretted en went on wuss 'n he did de night befo'. De nex' day his little eyes 'mence' ter lose dey shine, en he would n' eat nuffin, en he 'mence' ter look so peaked dat Aun' Nancy tuk 'n kyared 'im up ter de big house, en showed 'im ter her ole missis, en her ole missis gun her some med'cine fer 'im, en 'lowed ef he did n' git no better she sh'd fetch 'im up ter de big house ag'in, en dey'd hab a doctor, en nuss little Mose up dere. Fer Aun' Nancy's ole missis 'lowed he wuz a lackly little nigger en wu'th raisin'.

"But Aun' Nancy had l'arn' ter lack little Mose, en she did n' wanter hab 'im tuk up ter de big house. En so w'en he did n' git no better, she gethered a mess er green peas, and tuk de peas en de baby, en went ter see ole Aun' Peggy, de cunjuh 'oman down by de Wim'l'ton Road. She gun Aun' Peggy de mess er peas, en tol' her all 'bout Sis' Becky en little Mose.

"'Dat is a monst'us small mess er peas you is fotch' me,' sez Aun' Peggy, sez she.

"'Yas, I knows,' 'lowed Aun' Nancy, 'but dis yere is a monst'us small pickaninny.'

"'You'll hafter fetch me sump'n mo',' sez Aun' Peggy, 'fer you can't 'spec' me ter was'e my time diggin' roots en wukkin' cunj'ation fer nuffin.'

"'All right,' sez Aun' Nancy, 'I'll fetch you sump'n mo' nex' time.'

"'You bettah,' sez Aun' Peggy, 'er e'se dey'll be trouble. Wat dis yer little pickaninny needs is ter see his mammy. You leabe 'im heah 'tel ebenin' en I'll show 'im his mammy.'

"So w'en Aun' Nancy had gone 'way, Aun' Peggy tuk 'n wukked her roots, en tu'nt little Mose ter a hummin'-bird, en sont 'im off fer ter fin' his mammy.

"So little Mose flewed, en flewed, en flewed away, 'tel bimeby he got ter de place whar Sis' Becky b'longed. He seed his mammy wukkin' roun' de ya'd, en he could tell fum lookin' at her dat she wuz trouble' in her min' 'bout sump'n, en feelin' kin' er po'ly. Sis' Becky heared sump'n hummin' roun' en roun' her, sweet en low. Fus' she 'lowed it wuz a hummin'-bird; den she thought it sounded lack her little Mose croonin' on her breas' way back yander on de ole plantation. En she des 'magine' it wuz her little Mose, en it made her feel bettah, en she went on 'bout her wuk pearter 'n she'd done since she 'd be'n down dere. Little Mose stayed roun' 'tel late in de ebenin', en den flewed back ez hard ez he could ter Aun' Peggy. Ez fer Sis' Becky, she dremp all dat night dat she wuz holdin' her pickaninny in her arms, en kissin' him, en nussin' him, des lack she useter do back on de ole plantation whar he wuz bawn. En fer th'ee er fo' days Sis' Becky went 'bout her wuk wid mo' sperrit dan she 'd showed since she 'd be'n down dere ter dis man's plantation.

"De nex' day atter he come back, little Mose wuz mo' pearter en better 'n he had be'n fer a long time. But to'ds de een' er de week he 'mence' ter git res'less ag'in, en stop' eatin', en Aun' Nancy kyared 'im down ter Aun' Peggy once mo', en she tu'nt 'im ter a mawkin'-bird dis time, en sont 'im off ter see his mammy ag'in.

"It didn' take him long fer ter git dere, en w'en he did, he seed his mammy standin' in de kitchen, lookin' back in de d'rection little Mose wuz comin' fum. En dey wuz tears in her eyes, en she look' mo' po'ly en peaked 'n she had w'en he wuz down dere befo'. So little Mose sot on a tree in de ya'd en sung, en sung, en sung, des fittin' ter split his th'oat. Fus' Sis' Becky did n' notice 'im much, but dis mawkin'-bird kep' stayin' roun' de house all day, en bimeby Sis' Becky des 'magine' dat mawkin'-bird wuz her little Mose crowin' en crowin', des lack he useter do w'en his mammy would come home at night fum de cotton-fiel'. De mawkin'-bird stayed roun' dere 'mos' all day, en w'en Sis' Becky went out in de ya'd one time, dis yer mawkin'-bird lit on her shoulder en peck' at de piece er bread she wuz eatin', en fluttered his wings so dey rub' up agin de side er her head. En w'en he flewed away 'long late in de ebenin', des 'fo' sundown, Sis' Becky felt mo' better 'n she had sence she had heared dat hummin'-bird a week er so pas'. En dat night she dremp 'bout ole times ag'in, des lack she did befo'.

"But dis yer totin' little Mose down ter ole Aun' Peggy, en dis yer gittin' things fer ter pay de cunjuh 'oman, use' up a lot er Aun' Nancy's time, en she begun ter git kinder ti'ed. 'Sides dat, w'en Sis' Becky had be'n on de plantation, she had useter he'p Aun' Nancy wid de young uns ebenin's en Sundays; en Aun' Nancy 'mence' ter miss 'er monst'us, 'speshly sence she got a tech er de rheumatiz herse'f, en so she 'lows ter ole Aun' Peggy one day:—

"'Aun' Peggy, ain' dey no way you kin fetch Sis' Becky back home?'

"'Huh!' sez Aun' Peggy, 'I dunno 'bout dat. I'll hafter wuk my roots en fin' out whuther I kin er no. But it'll take a monst'us heap er wuk, en I can't was'e my time fer nuffin. Ef you'll fetch me sump'n ter pay me fer my trouble, I reckon we kin fix it.'

"So nex' day Aun' Nancy went down ter see Aun' Peggy ag'in.

"'Aun' Peggy,' sez she, 'I is fotch' you my bes' Sunday head-hankercher. Will dat do?'

"Aun' Peggy look' at de head-hankercher, en run her han' ober it, en sez she:—

"'Yas, dat'll do fus'-rate. I's be'n wukkin' my roots sence you be'n gone, en I 'lows mos' lackly I kin git Sis' Becky back, but it's gwine take fig'rin' en studyin' ez well ez cunj'in'. De fus' thing ter do'll be ter stop fetchin' dat pickaninny down heah, en not sen' 'im ter see his mammy no mo'. Ef he gits too po'ly, you lemme know, en I'll gib you some kin' er mixtry fer ter make 'im fergit Sis' Becky fer a week er so. So 'less'n you comes fer dat, you neenter come back ter see me no mo' 'tel I sen's fer you.'

"So Aun' Peggy sont Aun' Nancy erway, en de fus' thing she done wuz ter call a hawnet fum a nes' unner her eaves.

"'You go up ter Kunnel Pen'leton's stable, hawnet,' sez she, 'en sting de knees er de race hoss name' Lightnin' Bug. Be sho' en git de right one.'

"So de hawnet flewed up ter Kunnel Pen'leton's stable en stung Lightnin' Bug roun' de laigs, en de nex' mawnin' Lightnin' Bug's knees wuz all swoll' up, twice't ez big ez dey oughter be. W'en Kunnel Pen'leton went out ter de stable en see de hoss's laigs, hit would 'a' des made you trimble lack a leaf fer ter heah him cuss dat hoss trader. Howsomeber, he cool' off bimeby en tol' de stable boy fer ter rub Lightnin' Bug's laigs wid some linimum. De boy done ez his marster tol' 'im, en by de nex' day de swellin' had gone down consid'able. Aun' Peggy had sont a sparrer, w'at had a nes' in one er de trees close ter her cabin, fer ter watch w'at wuz gwine on 'roun' de big house, en w'en dis yer sparrer tol' 'er de hoss wuz gittin' ober de swellin', she sont de hawnet back fer ter sting 'is knees some mo', en de nex' mawnin' Lightnin' Bug's laigs wuz swoll' up wuss 'n befo'.

"Well, dis time Kunnel Pen'leton wuz mad th'oo en th'oo, en all de way 'roun', en he cusst dat hoss trader up en down, fum *A* ter *Izzard*. He cusst so ha'd dat de stable boy got mos' skeered ter def, en went off en hid hisse'f in de hay.

"Ez fer Kunnel Pen'leton, he went right up ter de house en got out his pen en ink, en tuk off his coat en roll' up his sleeves, en writ a letter ter dis yer hoss trader, en sezee:—

"'You is sol' me a hoss w'at is got a ringbone er a spavin er sump'n, en w'at I paid you fer wuz a soun' hoss. I wants you ter sen' my nigger 'oman back en take yo' ole hoss, er e'se I'll sue you, sho 's you bawn.'

"But dis yer man wa'n't skeered a bit, en he writ back ter Kunnel Pen'leton dat a bahg'in wuz a bahg'in; dat Lightnin' Bug wuz soun' w'en he sol' 'im, en ef Kunnel Pen'leton did n' knowed ernuff 'bout hosses ter take keer er a fine racer, dat wuz his own fune'al. En he say Kunnel Pen'leton kin sue en be cusst fer all he keer, but he ain' gwine ter gib up de nigger he bought en paid fer.

"W'en Kunnel Pen'leton got dis letter he wuz madder 'n he wuz befo', 'speshly 'ca'se dis man 'lowed he did n' know how ter take keer er fine hosses. But he could n' do nuffin but fetch a lawsuit, en he knowed, by his own 'spe'ience, dat lawsuits wuz slow ez de seben-yeah eetch en cos' mo' d'n dey come ter, en he 'lowed he better go slow en wait awhile.

"Aun' Peggy knowed w'at wuz gwine on all dis time, en she fix' up a little bag wid some roots en one thing en ernudder in it, en gun it ter dis sparrer er her'n, en tol' 'im ter take it 'way down yander whar Sis' Becky wuz, en drap it right befo' de do' er her cabin, so she 'd be sho' en fin' it de fus' time she come out'n de do'.

"One night Sis' Becky dremp' her pickaninny wuz dead, en de nex' day she wuz mo'nin' en groanin' all day. She dremp' de same dream th'ee nights runnin', en den, de nex' mawnin' atter de las' night, she foun' dis yer little bag de sparrer had drap' in front her do'; en she 'lowed she 'd be'n cunju'd, en wuz gwine ter die, en ez long ez her pickaninny wuz dead dey wa'n't no use tryin' ter do nuffin nohow. En so she tuk 'n went ter bed, en tol' her marster she 'd be'n cunju'd en wuz gwine ter die.

"Her marster lafft at her, en argyed wid her, en tried ter 'suade her out'n dis yer fool notion, ez he called it,—fer he wuz one er dese yer w'ite folks w'at purten' dey doan b'liebe in cunj'in',—but hit wa'n't no use. Sis' Becky kep' gittin' wusser en wusser, 'tel fin'lly dis yer man 'lowed Sis' Becky wuz gwine ter die, sho' 'nuff. En ez he knowed dey had n' be'n nuffin de matter wid Lightnin' Bug w'en he traded 'im, he 'lowed mebbe he could kyo' 'im en fetch 'im roun' all right, leas'ways good 'nuff ter sell ag'in. En anyhow, a lame hoss wuz better 'n a dead nigger. So he sot down en writ Kunnel Pen'leton a letter.

"'My conscience,' sezee, 'has be'n troublin' me 'bout dat ringbone' hoss I sol' you. Some folks 'lows a hoss trader ain' got no conscience, but dey doan know me, fer dat is my weak spot, en de reason I ain' made no mo' money hoss tradin'. Fac' is,' sezee, 'I is got so I can't sleep nights fum studyin' 'bout dat spavin' hoss; en I is made up my min' dat, w'iles a bahg'in is a bahg'in, en you seed Lightnin' Bug befo' you traded fer 'im, principle is wuth mo' d'n money er hosses er niggers. So ef you'll sen' Lightnin' Bug down heah, I'll sen' yo' nigger 'oman back, en we'll call de trade off, en be ez good frien's ez we eber wuz, en no ha'd feelin's.'

"So sho' 'nuff, Kunnel Pen'leton sont de hoss back. En w'en de man w'at come ter bring Lightnin' Bug tol' Sis' Becky her pickaninny wa'n't dead, Sis' Becky wuz so glad dat she 'lowed she wuz gwine ter try ter lib 'tel she got back whar she could see little Mose once mo'. En w'en she retch' de ole plantation en seed her baby kickin' en crowin' en holdin' out his little arms to'ds her, she wush' she wuz n' cunju'd en did n' hafter die. En w'en Aun' Nancy tol' 'er all 'bout Aun' Peggy, Sis' Becky went down ter see de cunjuh 'oman, en Aun' Peggy tol' her she had cunju'd her. En den Aun' Peggy tuk de goopher off'n her, en she got well, en stayed on de plantation, en raise' her pickaninny. En w'en little Mose growed up, he could sing en whistle des lack a mawkin'-bird, so dat de w'ite folks useter hab 'im come up ter de big house at night, en whistle en sing fer 'em, en dey useter gib 'im money en vittles en one thing er ernudder, w'ich he alluz tuk home ter his mammy; fer he knowed all 'bout w'at she had gone th'oo. He tu'nt out ter be a sma't man, en l'arnt de blacksmif trade; en Kunnel Pen'leton let 'im hire his time. En bimeby he bought his mammy en sot her free, en den he bought hisse'f, en tuk keer er Sis' Becky ez long ez dey bofe libbed."

My wife had listened to this story with greater interest than she had manifested in any subject for several days. I had watched her furtively from time to time during the recital, and had observed the play of her countenance. It had expressed in turn sympathy, indignation, pity, and at the end lively satisfaction.

"That is a very ingenious fairy tale, Julius," I said, "and we are much obliged to you."

"Why, John!" said my wife severely, "the story bears the stamp of truth, if ever a story did."

"Yes," I replied, "especially the humming-bird episode, and the mocking-bird digression, to say nothing of the doings of the hornet and the sparrow."

"Oh, well, I don't care," she rejoined, with delightful animation; "those are mere ornamental details and not at all essential. The story is true to nature, and might have happened half a hundred times, and no doubt did happen, in those horrid days before the war."

"By the way, Julius," I remarked, "your story doesn't establish what you started out to prove,—that a rabbit's foot brings good luck."

"Hit's plain 'nuff ter me, suh," replied Julius. "I bet young missis dere kin 'splain it herse'f."

"I rather suspect," replied my wife promptly, "that Sis' Becky had no rabbit's foot."

"You is hit de bull's-eye de fus' fire, ma'm," assented Julius. "Ef Sis' Becky had had a rabbit foot, she nebber would 'a' went th'oo all dis trouble."

I went into the house for some purpose, and left Julius talking to my wife. When I came back a moment later, he was gone.

My wife's condition took a turn for the better from this very day, and she was soon on the way to ultimate recovery. Several weeks later, after she had resumed her afternoon drives, which had been interrupted by her illness, Julius brought the rockaway round to the front door one day, and I assisted my wife into the carriage.

"John," she said, before I had taken my seat, "I wish you would look in my room, and bring me my handkerchief. You will find it in the pocket of my blue dress."

I went to execute the commission. When I pulled the handkerchief out of her pocket, something else came with it and fell on the floor. I picked up the object and looked at it. It was Julius's rabbit's foot.

CHARLES W. CHESNUTT

# The Gray Wolfs Ha'nt

I t was a rainy day at the vineyard. The morning had dawned bright and clear. But the sky had soon clouded, and by nine o'clock there was a light shower, followed by others at brief intervals. By noon the rain had settled into a dull, steady downpour. The clouds hung low, and seemed to grow denser instead of lighter as they discharged their watery burden, and there was now and then a muttering of distant thunder. Outdoor work was suspended, and I spent most of the day at the house, looking over my accounts and bringing up some arrears of correspondence.

Towards four o'clock I went out on the piazza, which was broad and dry, and less gloomy than the interior of the house, and composed myself for a quiet smoke. I had lit my cigar and opened the volume I was reading at that time, when my wife, whom I had left dozing on a lounge, came out and took a rocking-chair near me.

"I wish you would talk to me, or read to me—or something," she exclaimed petulantly. "It's awfully dull here today."

"I'll read to you with pleasure," I replied, and began at the point where I had found my bookmark:—

"'The difficulty of dealing with transformations so many-sided as those which all existences have undergone, or are undergoing, is such as to make a complete and deductive interpretation almost hopeless. So to grasp the total process of redistribution of matter and motion as to see simultaneously its several necessary results in their actual interdependence is scarcely possible. There is, however, a mode of rendering the process as a whole tolerably comprehensible. Though the genesis of the rearrangement of every evolving aggregate is in itself one, it presents to our intelligence'"—

"John," interrupted my wife, "I wish you would stop reading that nonsense and see who that is coming up the lane."

I closed my book with a sigh. I had never been able to interest my wife in the study of philosophy, even when presented in the simplest and most lucid form.

Some one was coming up the lane; at least, a huge faded cotton umbrella was making progress toward the house, and beneath it a pair of nether extremities in trousers was discernible. Any doubt in my mind as to whose they were was soon resolved when Julius reached the steps and, putting the umbrella down, got a good dash of the rain as he stepped up on the porch.

"Why in the world, Julius," I asked, "didn't you keep the umbrella up until you got under cover?"

"It's bad luck, suh, ter raise a' umbrella in de house, en w'iles I dunno whuther it's bad luck ter kyar one inter de piazzer er no, I 'lows it's alluz bes' ter be on de safe side. I did n' s'pose you en young missis 'u'd be gwine on yo' dribe ter-day, but bein' ez it's my pa't ter take you ef you does, I 'lowed I 'd repo't fer dooty, en let you say whuther er no you wants ter go."

"I'm glad you came, Julius," I responded. "We don't want to go driving, of course, in the rain, but I should like to consult you about another matter. I'm thinking of taking in a piece of new ground. What do you imagine it would cost to have that neck of woods down by the swamp cleared up?"

The old man's countenance assumed an expression of unwonted seriousness, and he shook his head doubtfully.

"I dunno 'bout dat, suh. It mought cos' mo', en it mought cos' less, ez fuh ez money is consarned. I ain' denyin' you could cl'ar up dat trac' er lan' fer a hund'ed er a couple er hund'ed dollahs,—ef you wants ter cl'ar it up. But ef dat 'uz my trac' er lan', I would n' 'sturb it, no, suh, I would n'; sho 's you bawn, I would n'."

"But why not?" I asked.

"It ain' fittin' fer grapes, fer noo groun' nebber is."

"I know it, but"—

"It ain' no yeathly good fer cotton, 'ca'se it's top low."

"Perhaps so; but it will raise splendid corn."

"I dunno," rejoined Julius deprecatorily. "It's so nigh de swamp dat de 'coons'll eat up all de cawn."

"I think I'll risk it," I answered.

"Well, suh," said Julius, "I wushes you much joy er yo' job. Ef you has bad luck er sickness er trouble er any kin', doan blame *me*. You can't say ole Julius did n' wa'n you."

"Warn him of what, Uncle Julius?" asked my wife.

"Er de bad luck w'at follers folks w'at 'sturbs dat trac' er lan'. Dey is snakes en sco'pions in dem woods. En ef you manages ter 'scape de p'isen animals, you is des boun' ter hab a ha'nt ter settle wid,—ef you doan hab two."

"Whose haunt?" my wife demanded, with growing interest.

"De gray wolf's ha'nt, some folks calls it,—but I knows better."

"Tell us about it, Uncle Julius," said my wife. "A story will be a godsend to-day."

It was not difficult to induce the old man to tell a story, if he were in a reminiscent mood. Of tales of the old slavery days he seemed indeed to possess an exhaustless store,—some weirdly grotesque, some broadly humorous; some bearing the stamp of truth, faint, perhaps, but still discernible; others palpable inventions, whether his own or not we never knew, though his fancy doubtless embellished them. But even the wildest was not without an element of pathos,—the tragedy, it might be, of the story itself; the shadow, never absent, of slavery and of ignorance; the sadness, always, of life as seen by the fading light of an old man's memory.

"Way back yander befo' de wah," began Julius, "ole Mars Dugal' McAdoo useter own a nigger name' Dan. Dan wuz big en strong en hearty en peaceable en good-nachu'd most er de time, but dange'ous ter aggervate. He alluz done his task, en nebber had no trouble wid de w'ite folks, but woe be unter de nigger w'at 'lowed he c'd fool wid Dan, fer he wuz mos' sho' ter git a good lammin'. Soon ez eve'ybody foun' Dan out, dey did n' many un 'em 'temp' ter 'sturb 'im. De one dat did would 'a' wush' he had n', ef he could 'a' libbed long ernuff ter do any wushin'.

"It all happen' dis erway. Dey wuz a cunjuh man w'at libbed ober t' other side er de Lumbe'ton Road. He had be'n de only cunjuh doctor in de naberhood fer lo! dese many yeahs, 'tel ole Aun' Peggy sot up in de bizness down by de Wim'l'ton Road. Dis cunjuh man had a son w'at libbed wid 'im, en it wuz dis yer son w'at got mix' up wid Dan,—en all 'bout a 'oman.

"Dey wuz a gal on de plantation name' Mahaly. She wuz a monst'us lackly gal,—tall en soopl', wid big eyes, en a small foot, en a lively tongue, en w'en Dan tuk ter gwine wid 'er eve'ybody 'lowed dey wuz well match', en none er de yuther nigger men on de plantation das' ter go nigh her, fer dey wuz all feared er Dan.

"Now, it happen' dat dis yer cunjuh man's son wuz gwine 'long de road one day, w'en who sh'd come pas' but Mahaly. En de minute dis man sot eyes on Mahaly, he 'lowed he wuz gwine ter hab her fer hisse'f. He come up side er her en 'mence' ter talk ter her; but she didn' paid no 'tention ter 'im, fer she wuz studyin' 'bout Dan, en she did n' lack dis nigger's looks nohow. So w'en she got ter whar she wuz gwine, dis yer man wa'n't no fu'ther 'long dan he wuz w'en he sta'ted.

"Co'se, atter he had made up his min' fer ter git Mahaly, he 'mence' ter 'quire 'roun', en soon foun' out all 'bout Dan, en w'at a dange'ous nigger he wuz. But dis man 'lowed his daddy wuz a cunjuh man, en so he 'd come out all right in de een'; en he kep' right on atter Mahaly. Meanw'iles Dan's marster had said dey could git married ef dey wanter, en so Dan en Mahaly had tuk up wid one ernudder, en wuz libbin' in a cabin by deyse'ves, en wuz des wrop' up in one ernudder.

"But dis yer cunjuh man's son did n' 'pear ter min' Dan's takin' up wid Mahaly, en he kep' on hangin' 'roun' des de same, 'tel fin'lly one day Mahaly sez ter Dan, sez she:—

"'I wush you 'd do sump'n ter stop dat free nigger man fum follerin' me 'roun'. I doan lack him nohow, en I ain' got no time fer ter was'e wid no man but you.'

"Co'se Dan got mad w'en he heared 'bout dis man pest'rin' Mahaly, en de nex' night, w'en he seed dis nigger comin' 'long de road, he up en ax' 'im w'at he mean by hangin' 'roun' his 'oman. De man did n' 'spon' ter suit Dan, en one wo'd led ter ernudder, 'tel bimeby dis cunjuh man's son pull' out a knife en sta'ted ter stick it in Dan; but befo' he could git it drawed good, Dan haul' off en hit 'im in de head so ha'd dat he nebber got up. Dan 'lowed he 'd come to atter a w'ile en go 'long 'bout his bizness, so he went off en lef' 'im layin' dere on de groun'.

"De nex' mawnin' de man wuz foun' dead. Dey wuz a great 'miration made 'bout it, but Dan did n' say nuffin, en none er de yuther niggers had n' seed de fight, so dey wa'n't no way ter tell who done de killin'. En bein' ez it wuz a free nigger, en dey wa'n't no w'ite folks 'speshly int'rusted, dey wa'n't nuffin done 'bout it, en de cunjuh man come en tuk his son en kyared 'im 'way en buried 'im.

"Now, Dan had n' meant ter kill dis nigger, en w'iles he knowed de man had n'' got no mo' d'n he desarved, Dan 'mence' ter worry mo' er less. Fer he knowed dis man's daddy would wuk his roots en prob'ly fin' out who had killt 'is son, en make all de trouble fer 'im he could. En Dan kep' on studyin' 'bout dis 'tel he got so he did n' ha'dly das' ter eat er drink fer fear dis cunjuh man had p'isen' de vittles er de water. Fin'lly he 'lowed he 'd go ter see Aun' Peggy, de noo cunjuh 'oman w'at had moved down by de Wim'l'ton Road, en ax her fer ter do sump'n ter pertec' 'im fum dis cunjuh man. So he tuk a peck er 'taters en went down ter her cabin one night.

"Aun' Peggy heared his tale, en den sez she:—

"'Dat cunjuh man is mo' d'n twice't ez ole ez I is, en he kin make monst'us powe'ful goopher. W'at you needs is a life-cha'm, en I'll make you one ter-morrer; it's de on'y thing w'at'll do you any good. You leabe me a couple er ha'rs fum yo' head, en fetch me a pig ter-morrer night fer ter roas', en w'en you come I'll hab de cha'm all ready fer you.'

"So Dan went down ter Aun' Peggy de nex' night,—wid a young shote,—en Aun' Peggy gun 'im de cha'm. She had tuk de ha'rs Dan had lef wid 'er, en a piece er red flannin, en some roots en yarbs, en had put 'em in a little bag made out'n 'coon-skin.

"'You take dis cha'm,' sez she, 'en put it in a bottle er a tin box, en bury it deep unner de root er a live-oak tree, en ez long ez it stays dere safe en soun', dey ain' no p'isen kin p'isen you, dey ain' no rattlesnake kin bite you, dey ain' no sco'pion kin sting you. Dis yere cunjuh man mought do one thing er 'nudder ter you, but he can't kill you. So you neenter be at all skeered, but go 'long 'bout yo' bizness en doan bother yo' min'.'

"So Dan went down by de ribber, en 'way up on de bank he buried de cha'm deep unner de root er a live-oak tree, en kivered it up en stomp' de dirt down en scattered leaves ober de spot, en den went home wid his min' easy.

"Sho' 'nuff, dis yer cunjuh man wukked his roots, des ez Dan had 'spected he would, en soon l'arn' who killt his son. En co'se he made up his min' fer ter git eben wid Dan. So he sont a rattlesnake fer ter sting 'im, but de rattlesnake say de nigger's heel wuz so ha'd he could n' git his sting in. Den he sont his jay-bird fer ter put p'isen in Dan's vittles, but de p'isen did n' wuk. Den de cunjuh man 'low' he'd double Dan all up wid de rheumatiz, so he could n' git 'is ban' ter his mouf ter eat, en would hafter sta've ter def; but Dan went ter Aun' Peggy, en she gun 'im a' 'intment ter kyo de rheumatiz. Den de cunjuh man 'lowed he 'd bu'n Dan up wid a fever, but Aun' Peggy tol' 'im how ter make some yarb tea fer dat. Nuffin dis man tried would kill Dan, so fin'lly de cunjuh man 'lowed Dan mus' hab a life-cha'm.

"Now, dis yer jay-bird de cunjuh man had wuz a monst'us sma't creeter,—fac', de niggers 'lowed he wuz de ole Debbil hisse'f, des settin' roun' waitin' ter kyar dis ole man erway w'en he 'd retch' de een' er his rope. De cunjuh man sont dis jay-bird fer ter watch Dan en fin' out whar he kep' his cha'm. De jay-bird hung roun' Dan fer a week er so, en one day he seed Dan go down by de ribber en look at a live-oak tree; en den de jay-bird went back ter his marster, en tol' 'im he 'spec' de nigger kep' his life-cha'm under dat tree.

"De cunjuh man lafft en lafft, en he put on his bigges' pot, en fill' it wid his stronges' roots, en b'iled it en b'iled it, 'tel bimeby de win' blowed en blowed, 'tel it blowed down de live-oak tree. Den he stirred some more roots in de pot, en it rained en rained 'tel de water run down de ribber bank en wash' Dan's life-cha'm inter de ribber, en de bottle went bobbin' down de current des ez onconsarned ez ef it wa'n't takin' po' Dan's chances all 'long wid it. En den de cunjuh man lafft some mo', en 'lowed ter hisse'f dat he wuz gwine ter fix Dan now, sho' 'nuff; he wa'n't gwine ter kill 'im des yet, fer he could do sump'n ter 'im w'at would hu't wusser 'n killin'.

"So dis cunjuh man 'mence' by gwine up ter Dan's cabin eve'y night, en takin' Dan out in his sleep en ridin' 'im roun' de roads en fiel's ober de rough groun'. In de mawnin' Dan would be ez ti'ed ez ef he had n' be'n ter sleep. Dis kin' er thing kep' up fer a week er so, en Dan had des 'bout made up his min' fer ter go en see Aun' Peggy ag'in, w'en who sh'd he come across, gwine 'long de road one day, to'ds sundown, but dis yer cunjuh man. Dan felt kinder skeered at fus'; but den he 'membered 'bout his life-cha'm, w'ich he had n' be'n ter see fer a week er so, en 'lowed wuz safe en soun' unner de live-oak tree, en so he hilt up 'is head en walk' 'long, des lack he did n' keer nuffin 'bout dis man no mo' d'n any yuther nigger. Wen he got close ter de cunjuh man, dis cunjuh man sez, sezee:—

"'Hoddy, Brer Dan? I hopes you er well?'

"Wen Dan seed de cunjuh man wuz in a good humor en did n' 'pear ter bear no malice, Dan 'lowed mebbe de cunjuh man had n' foun' out who killt his son, en so he 'termine' fer ter let on lack he did n' know nuffin, en so sezee:—

"'Hoddy, Unk' Jube?'—dis ole cunjuh man's name wuz Jube. 'I 's p'utty well, I thank you. How is you feelin' dis mawnin'?'

"'I's feelin' ez well ez a' ole nigger could feel w'at had los' his only son, en his main 'pen'ence in 'is ole age.

"'But den my son wuz a bad boy,' sezee, 'en I could n' 'spec' nuffin e'se. I tried ter l'arn him de arrer er his ways en make him go ter chu'ch en pra'r-meetin'; but it wa'n't no use. I dunno who killt 'im, en I doan wanter know, fer I 'd be mos' sho' ter fin' out dat my boy had sta'ted de fuss. Ef I 'd 'a' had a son lack you, Brer Dan, I 'd 'a' be'n a proud nigger; oh, yas, I would, sho's you bawn. But you ain' lookin' ez well ez you oughter, Brer Dan. Dey's sump'n de matter wid you, en w'at 's mo', I 'spec' you dunno w'at it is.'

CHARLES W. CHESNUTT

"Now, dis yer kin' er talk nach'ly th'owed Dan off'n his gya'd, en fus' thing he knowed he wuz talkin' ter dis ole cunjuh man des lack he wuz one er his bes' frien's. He tol' 'im all 'bout not feelin' well in de mawnin', en ax' 'im ef he could tell w'at wuz de matter wid 'im.

"'Yas,' sez de cunjuh man. 'Dey is a witch be'n ridin' you right 'long. I kin see de marks er de bridle on yo' mouf. En I'll des bet yo' back is raw whar she's be'n beatin' you.'

"'Yas,' 'spon' Dan, 'so it is.' He had n' notice it befo', but now he felt des lack de hide had be'n tuk off'n 'im.

"'En yo' thighs is des raw whar de spurrers has be'n driv' in you,' sez de cunjuh man. 'You can't see de raw spots, but you kin feel 'em.'

"'Oh, yas,' 'lows Dan, 'dey does hu't pow'ful bad.'

"'En w'at's mo',' sez de cunjuh man, comin' up close ter Dan en whusp'in' in his yeah, 'I knows who it is be'n ridin' you.'

"'Who is it?' ax' Dan. 'Tell me who it is.'

"'It's a' ole nigger 'oman down by Rockfish Crick. She had a pet rabbit, en you cotch' 'im one day, en she's been squarin' up wid you eber sence. But you better stop her, er e'se you'll be rid ter def in a mont' er so.'

"'No,' sez Dan, 'she can't kill me, sho'.'

"'I dunno how dat is,' said de cunjuh man, 'but she kin make yo' life mighty mis'able. Ef I wuz in yo' place, I'd stop her right off.'

"'But how is I gwine ter stop her?' ax' Dan. 'I dunno nuffin 'bout stoppin' witches.'

"'Look a heah, Dan,'sez de yuther; 'you is a goad young man. I lacks you monst'us well. Fac', I feels lack some er dese days I mought buy you fum yo' marster, ef I could eber make money ernuff at my bizness dese hard times, en 'dop' you fer my son. I lacks you so well dat I'm gwine ter he'p you git rid er dis yer witch fer good en all; fer des ez long ez she libs, you is sho' ter hab trouble, en trouble, en mo' trouble.'

"'You is de bes' frien' I got, Unk' Jube,' sez Dan, 'en I'll 'member yo' kin'ness ter my dyin' day. Tell me how I kin git rid er dis yer ole witch w'at's be'n ridin' me so ha'd.'

"'In de fus' place,' sez de cunjuh man, 'dis ole witch nebber comes in her own shape, but eve'y night, at ten o'clock, she tu'ns herse'f inter a black cat, en runs down ter yo' cabin en bridles you, en mounts you, en dribes you out th'oo de chimbly, en rides you ober de roughes' places she kin fin'. All you got ter do is ter set fer her in de bushes 'side er yo' cabin, en hit her in de head wid a rock er a lighterd-knot w'en she goes pas'.'

"'But,' sez Dan, 'how kin I see her in de da'k? En s'posen I hits at her en misses her? Er s'posen I des woun's her, en she gits erway,—w'at she gwine do ter me den?'

"'I is done studied 'bout all dem things,' sez de cunjuh man, 'en it 'pears ter me de bes' plan fer you ter foller is ter lemme tu'n you ter some creetur w'at kin see in de da'k, en w'at kin run des ez fas' ez a cat, en w'at kin bite, en bite fer ter kill; en den you won't hafter hab no trouble atter de job is done. I dunno whuther you'd lack dat er no, but dat is de sho'es' way.'

"'I doan keer,' 'spon' Dan. 'I'd des ez lief be anything fer a' hour er so, ef I kin kill dat ole witch. You kin do des w'at you er mineter.'

"'All right, den,' sez de cunjuh man, 'you come down ter my cabin at half-past nine o'clock ter-night, en I'll fix you up.'

"Now, dis cunjuh man, w'en he had got th'oo talkin' wid Dan, kep' on down de road 'long de side er de plantation, 'tel he met Mahaly comin' home fum wuk des atter sundown.

"'Hoddy do, ma'm,' sezee; 'is yo' name Sis' Mahaly, w'at b'longs ter Mars Dugal' McAdoo?'

"'Yas,' 'spon' Mahaly, 'dat's my name, en I b'longs ter Mars Dugal'.'

"'Well,' sezee, 'yo' husban' Dan wuz down by my cabin dis ebenin', en he got bit by a spider er sump'n, en his foot is swoll' up so he can't walk. En he ax' me fer ter fin' you en fetch you down dere ter he'p 'im home.'

"Co'se Mahaly wanter see w'at had happen' ter Dan, en so she sta'ted down de road wid de cunjuh man. Ez soon ez he got her inter his cabin, he shet de do', en sprinkle' some goopher mixtry on her, en tu'nt her ter a black cat. Den he tuk 'n put her in a bairl, en put a bo'd on de bairl, en a rock on de bo'd, en lef' her dere 'tel he got good en ready fer ter use her.

"'Long 'bout half-pas' nine o'clock Dan come down ter de cunjuh man's cabin. It wuz a wa'm night, en de do' wuz stan'in' open. De cunjuh man 'vited Dan ter come in, en pass' de time er day wid 'im. Ez soon ez Dan 'mence' talkin', he heared a cat miauin' en scratchin' en gwine on at a tarrable rate.

"'Wat's all dat fuss 'bout?' ax' Dan.

"'Oh, dat ain' nuffin but my ole gray tomcat,' sez de cunjuh man. 'I has ter shet 'im up sometimes fer ter keep 'im in nights, en co'se he doan lack it.

"'Now,' 'lows de cunjuh man, 'lemme tell you des w'at you is got ter do. Wen you ketches dis witch, you mus' take her right by de th'oat en bite her right th'oo de neck. Be sho' yo' teef goes th'oo at de fus' bite, en den you won't nebber be bothe'd no mo' by dat witch. En w'en you git done, come back heah en I'll tu'n you ter yo'se'f ag'in, so you kin go home en git yo' night's res'.'

"Den de cunjuh man gun Dan sump'n nice en sweet ter drink out'n a new go'd, en in 'bout a minute Dan foun' hisse'f tu'nt ter a gray wolf; en soon ez he felt all fo' er his noo feet on de groun', he sta'ted off fas' ez he could fer his own cabin, so he could be sho' en be dere time ernuff ter ketch de witch, en put a' een' ter her kyarin's-on.

"Ez soon ez Dan wuz gone good, de cunjuh man tuk de rock off'n de bo'd, en de bo'd off'n de bairl, en out le'p' Mahaly en sta'ted fer ter go home, des lack a cat er a 'oman er anybody e'se would w'at wuz in trouble; en it wa'n't many minutes befo' she wuz gwine up de path ter her own do'.

"Meanw'iles, w'en Dan had retch' de cabin, he had hid hisse'f in a bunch er jimson weeds in de ya'd. He had n' wait' long befo' he seed a black cat run up de path to'ds de do'. Des ez soon ez she got close ter 'im, he le'p' out en ketch' her by de th'oat, en got a grip on her, des lack de cunjuh man had tol' 'im ter do. En lo en behol'! no sooner had de blood 'mence' ter flow dan de black cat tu'nt back ter Mahaly, en Dan seed dat he had killt his own wife. En w'iles her bref wuz gwine she call' out:

"'O Dan! O my husban'! come en he'p me! come en sabe me fum dis wolf w'at 's killin' me!'

"Wen po' Dan sta'ted to'ds her, ez any man nach'ly would, it des made her holler wuss en wuss; fer she did n' knowed dis yer wolf wuz her Dan. En Dan des had ter hide in de weeds, en grit his teef en hoi' hisse'f in, 'tel she passed out'n her mis'ry, callin' fer Dan ter de las', en wond'rin' w'y he did n' come en he'p her. En Dan 'lowed ter hisse'f he 'd ruther 'a' be'n killt a dozen times 'n ter 'a' done w'at he had ter Mahaly.

"Dan wuz mighty nigh 'stracted, but w'en Mahaly wuz dead en he got his min' straighten' out a little, it did n' take 'im mo' d'n a minute er so fer ter see th'oo all de cunjuh man's lies, en how de cunjuh man had fooled 'im en made 'im kill Mahaly, fer ter git eben wid 'im fer killin' er his son. He kep' gittin' madder en madder, en Mahaly had n' much mo' d'n drawed her' las bref befo' he sta'ted back ter de cunjuh man's cabin ha'd ez he could run.

"Wen he got dere, de do' wuz stan'in' open; a lighterd-knot wuz flick'rin' on de h'a'th, en de ole cunjuh man wuz settin' dere noddin' in de corner. Dan le'p' in de do' en jump' fer dis man's th'oat, en got de same grip on 'im w'at de cunjuh man had tol' 'im 'bout half a' hour befo'. It wuz ha'd wuk dis time, fer de ole man's neck wuz monst'us tough en stringy, but Dan hilt on long ernuff ter be sho' his job wuz done right. En eben den he did n' hol' on long ernuff; fer w'en he tu'nt de cunjuh man loose en he fell ober on de flo', de cunjuh man rollt his eyes at Dan, en sezee:—

"'I's eben wid you, Brer Dan, en you er eben wid me; you killt my son en I killt yo' 'oman. En ez I doan want no mo' d'n w'at 's fair 'bout dis thing, ef you'll retch up wid yo' paw en take down dat go'd hangin' on dat peg ober de chimbly, en take a sip er dat mixtry, it'll tu'n you back ter a nigger ag'in, en I kin die mo' sad'sfied 'n ef I lef you lack you is.'

"Dan nebber 'lowed fer a minute dat a man would lie wid his las' bref, en co'se he seed de sense er gittin' tu'nt back befo' de cunjuh man died; so he dumb on a chair en retch' fer de go'd, en tuk a sip er de mixtry. En ez soon ez he 'd done dat de cunjuh man lafft his las' laf, en gasped out wid 'is las' gaps:—

"'Uh huh! I reckon I's square wid you now fer killin' me, too; fer dat goopher on you is done fix' en sot now fer good, en all de cunj'in' in de worl' won't nebber take it off.

'Wolf you is en wolf you stays,
All de rest er yo' bawn days.'

"Co'se Brer Dan could n' do nuffin. He knowed it wa'n't no use, but he dumb up on de chimbly en got down de go'ds en bottles en yuther cunjuh fixin's, en tried 'em all on hisse'f, but dey didn' do no good. Den he run down ter ole Aun' Peggy, but she did n' know de wolf langwidge, en couldn't 'a' tuk off dis yuther goopher nohow, eben ef she 'd 'a' unnerstood w'at Dan wuz sayin'. So po' Dan wuz bleedgd ter be a wolf all de rest er his bawn days.

"Dey foun' Mahaly down by her own cabin nex' mawnin', en eve'ybody made a great 'miration 'bout how she 'd be'n killt. De niggers 'lowed a wolf had bit her. De w'ite folks say no, dey ain' be'n no wolves 'roun' dere fer ten yeahs er mo'; en dey did n' know w'at ter make out'n it. En w'en dey could n' fin' Dan nowhar, dey 'lowed he'd quo'lled wid Mahaly en killt her, en run erway; en dey did n' know w'at ter make er dat, fer Dan en Mahaly wuz de mos' lovin' couple on de plantation. Dey put de dawgs on Dan's scent, en track' 'im down ter ole Unk' Jube's cabin, en foun' de ole man dead, en dey did n' know w'at ter make er

CHARLES W. CHESNUTT

dat; en den Dan's scent gun out, en dey didn' know w'at ter make er dat. Mars Dugal' tuk on a heap 'bout losin' two er his bes' han's in one day, en ole missis 'lowed it wuz a jedgment on 'im fer sump'n he'd done. But dat fall de craps wuz monst'us big, so Mars Dugal' say de Lawd had temper' de win' ter de sho'n ram, en make up ter 'im fer w'at he had los'.

"Dey buried Mahaly down in dat piece er low groun' you er talkin' 'bout cl'arin' up. Ez fer po' Dan, he did n' hab nowhar e'se ter go, so he des stayed 'roun' Mahaly's grabe, w'en he wa'n't out in de yuther woods gittin' sump'n ter eat. En sometimes, w'en night would come, de niggers useter heah him howlin' en howlin' down dere, des fittin' ter break his hea't. En den some mo' un 'em said dey seed Mahaly's ha'nt dere 'bun'ance er times, colloguin' wid dis gray wolf. En eben now, fifty yeahs sence, long atter ole Dan has died en dried up in de woods, his ha'nt en Mahaly's hangs 'roun' dat piece er low groun', en eve'body w'at goes 'bout dere has some bad luck er 'nuther; fer ha'nts doan lack ter be 'sturb' on dey own stompin'-groun'."

The air had darkened while the old man related this harrowing tale. The rising wind whistled around the eaves, slammed the loose window-shutters, and, still increasing, drove the rain in fiercer gusts into the piazza. As Julius finished his story and we rose to seek shelter within doors, the blast caught the angle of some chimney or gable in the rear of the house, and bore to our ears a long, wailing note, an epitome, as it were, of remorse and hopelessness.

"Dat 's des lack po' ole Dan useter howl," observed Julius, as he reached for his umbrella, "en w'at I be'n tellin' you is de reason I doan lack ter see dat neck er woods cl'ared up. Co'se it b'longs ter you, en a man kin do ez he choose' wid 'is own. But ef you gits rheumatiz er fever en agur, er ef you er snake-bit er p'isen' wid some yarb er 'nuther, er ef a tree falls on you, er a ha'nt runs you en makes you git 'stracted in yo' min', lack some folks I knows w'at went foolin' 'roun' dat piece er lan', you can't say I neber wa'ned you, suh, en tol' you w'at you mought look fer en be sho' ter fin'."

When I cleared up the land in question, which was not until the following year, I recalled the story Julius had told us, and looked in vain for a sunken grave or perhaps a few weather-bleached bones of some denizen of the forest. I cannot say, of course, that some one had not been buried there; but if so, the hand of time had long since removed any evidence of the fact. If some lone wolf, the last of his pack, had once made his den there, his bones had long since crumbled into dust and gone to fertilize the rank vegetation that formed the undergrowth of this wild spot. I did find, however, a bee-tree in the woods, with an ample cavity in its trunk, and an opening through which convenient access could be had to the stores of honey within. I have reason to believe that ever since I had bought the place, and for many years before, Julius had been getting honey from this tree. The gray wolf's haunt had doubtless proved useful in keeping off too inquisitive people, who might have interfered with his monopoly.

# Hot-Foot Hannibal

I hate you and despise you! I wish never to see you or speak to you again!"

"Very well; I will take care that henceforth you have no opportunity to do either."

These words—the first in the passionately vibrant tones of my sister-in-law, and the latter in the deeper and more restrained accents of an angry man—startled me from my nap. I had been dozing in my hammock on the front piazza, behind the honeysuckle vine. I had been faintly aware of a buzz of conversation in the parlor, but had not at all awakened to its import until these sentences fell, or, I might rather say, were hurled upon my ear. I presume the young people had either not seen me lying there,—the Venetian blinds opening from the parlor windows upon the piazza were partly closed on account of the heat,— or else in their excitement they had forgotten my proximity.

I felt somewhat concerned. The young man, I had remarked, was proud, firm, jealous of the point of honor, and, from my observation of him, quite likely to resent to the bitter end what he deemed a slight or an injustice. The girl, I knew, was quite as high-spirited as young Murchison. I feared she was not so just, and hoped she would prove more yielding. I knew that her affections were strong and enduring, but that her temperament was capricious, and her sunniest moods easily overcast by some small cloud of jealousy or pique. I had never imagined, however, that she was capable of such intensity as was revealed by these few words of hers. As I say, I felt concerned. I had learned to like Malcolm Murchison, and had heartily consented to his marriage with my ward; for it was in that capacity that I had stood for a year or two to my wife's younger sister, Mabel. The match thus rudely broken off had promised to be another link binding me to the kindly Southern people among whom I had not long before taken up my residence.

Young Murchison came out of the door, cleared the piazza in two strides without seeming aware of my presence, and went off down the lane at a furious pace. A few moments later Mabel began playing the piano loudly, with a touch that indicated anger and pride and independence and a dash of exultation, as though she were really glad that she had driven away forever the young man whom the day before she had loved with all the ardor of a first passion.

I hoped that time might heal the breach and bring the two young people together again. I told my wife what I had overheard. In return she gave me Mabel's version of the affair.

"I do not see how it can ever be settled," my wife said. "It is something more than a mere lovers' quarrel. It began, it is true, because she found fault with him for going to church with that hateful Branson girl. But before it ended there were things said that no woman of any spirit could stand. I am afraid it is all over between them."

I was sorry to hear this. In spite of the very firm attitude taken by my wife and her sister, I still hoped that the quarrel would be made up within a day or two. Nevertheless, when a week had passed with no word from young Murchison, and with no sign of relenting on Mabel's part, I began to think myself mistaken.

One pleasant afternoon, about ten days after the rupture, old Julius drove the rockaway up to the piazza, and my wife, Mabel, and I took our seats for a drive to a neighbor's vineyard, over on the Lumberton plank-road.

"Which way shall we go," I asked,—"the short road or the long one?"

"I guess we had better take the short road," answered my wife. "We will get there sooner."

"It's a mighty fine dribe roun' by de big road, Mis' Annie," observed Julius, "en it doan take much longer to git dere."

"No," said my wife, "I think we will go by the short road. There is a bay-tree in blossom near the mineral spring, and I wish to get some of the flowers."

"I 'spec's you 'd fin' some bay-trees 'long de big road, ma'm," suggested Julius.

"But I know about the flowers on the short road, and they are the ones I want."

We drove down the lane to the highway, and soon struck into the short road leading past the mineral spring. Our route lay partly through a swamp, and on each side the dark, umbrageous foliage, unbroken by any clearing, lent to the road solemnity, and to the air a refreshing coolness. About half a mile from the house, and about half-way to the mineral spring, we stopped at the tree of which my wife had spoken, and reaching up to the low-hanging boughs, I gathered a dozen of the fragrant white flowers. When I resumed my seat in the rockaway, Julius started the mare. She went on for a few rods, until we had reached the edge of a branch crossing the road, when she stopped short.

CHARLES W. CHESNUTT

"Why did you stop, Julius?" I asked.

"I did n', suh," he replied. "'T wuz de mare stop'. G''long dere, Lucy! Wat you mean by dis foolis'ness?"

Julius jerked the reins and applied the whip lightly, but the mare did not stir.

"Perhaps you had better get down and lead her," I suggested. "If you get her started, you can cross on the log and keep your feet dry."

Julius alighted, took hold of the bridle, and vainly essayed to make the mare move. She planted her feet with even more evident obstinacy.

"I don't know what to make of this," I said. "I have never known her to balk before. Have you, Julius?"

"No, suh," replied the old man, "I neber has. It's a cu'ous thing ter me, suh."

"What's the best way to make her go?"

"I 'spec's, suh, dat ef I'd tu'n her 'roun', she'd go de udder way."

"But we want her to go this way."

"Well, suh, I 'low ef we des set heah fo' er fibe minutes, she'll sta't up by herse'f."

"All right," I rejoined; "it is cooler here than any place I have struck today. We'll let her stand for a while, and see what she does."

We had sat in silence for a few minutes, when Julius suddenly exclaimed, "Uh huh! I knows w'y dis mare doan go. It des flash' 'cross my recommemb'ance."

"Why is it, Julius?" I inquired.

"'Ca'se she sees Chloe."

"Where is Chloe?" I demanded.

"Chloe's done be'n dead dese fo'ty years er mo'," the old man returned. "Her ha'nt is settin' ober yander on de udder side er de branch, unner dat wilier-tree, dis blessed minute."

"Why, Julius!" said my wife, "do you see the haunt?"

"No'm," he answered, shaking his head, "I doan see 'er, but de mare sees 'er."

"How do you know?" I inquired.

"Well, suh, dis yer is a gray hoss, en dis yer is a Friday; en a gray hoss kin alluz see a ha'nt w'at walks on Friday."

"Who was Chloe?" said Mabel.

"And why does Chloe's haunt walk?" asked my wife.

"It's all in de tale, ma'm," Julius replied, with a deep sigh. "It's all in de tale."

"Tell us the tale," I said. "Perhaps, by the time you get through, the haunt will go away and the mare will cross."

I was willing to humor the old man's fancy. He had not told us a story for some time; and the dark and solemn swamp around us; the amber-colored stream flowing silently and sluggishly at our feet, like the waters of Lethe; the heavy, aromatic scent of the bays, faintly suggestive of funeral wreaths, all made the place an ideal one for a ghost story.

"Chloe," Julius began in a subdued tone, "use' ter b'long ter ole Mars' Dugal' McAdoo,—my ole marster. She wuz a lackly gal en a smart gal, en ole mis' tuk her up ter de big house, en l'arnt her ter wait on de w'ite folks, 'tel bimeby she come ter be mis's own maid, en 'peared ter 'low she run de house herse'f, ter heah her talk erbout it. I wuz a young boy den, en use' ter wuk 'bout de stables, so I knowed eve'ythin' dat wuz gwine on 'roun' de plantation.

"Well, one time Mars' Dugal' wanted a house boy, en sont down ter de qua'ters fer ter hab Jeff en Hannibal come up ter de big house nex' mawnin'. Ole marster en ole mis' look' de two boys ober, en 'sco'sed wid deyse'ves fer a little w'ile, en den Mars' Dugal' sez, sezee:—

"'We lacks Hannibal de bes', en we gwine ter keep him. Heah, Hannibal, you'll wuk at de house fum now on. En ef you er a good nigger en min's yo' bizness, I'll gib you Chloe fer a wife nex' spring. You other nigger, you Jeff, you kin go back ter de qua'ters. We ain' gwine ter need you.'

"Now Chloe had be'n stan'in' dere behin' ole mis' dyoin' all er dis yer talk, en Chloe made up her min' fum de ve'y fus' minute she sot eyes on dem two dat she did n' lack dat nigger Hannibal, en wa'n't neber gwine keer fer 'im, en she wuz des ez sho' dat she lack' Jeff, en wuz gwine ter set sto' by 'im, whuther Mars' Dugal' tuk 'im in de big house er no; en so co'se Chloe wuz monst'us sorry w'en ole Mars' Dugal' tuk Hannibal en sont Jeff back. So she slip' roun' de house en waylaid Jeff on de way back ter de qua'ters, en tol' 'im not ter be down-hea'ted, fer she wuz gwine ter see ef she could n' fin' some way er 'nuther ter git rid er dat nigger Hannibal, en git Jeff up ter de house in his place.

"De noo house boy kotch' on monst'us fas', en it wa'n't no time ha'dly befo' Mars' Dugal' en ole mis' bofe 'mence' ter 'low Hannibal wuz de bes' house boy dey eber had. He wuz peart en soopl', quick ez lightnin', en sha'p ez a razor. But Chloe did n' lack his ways. He wuz so sho' he wuz gwine ter git 'er in de spring, dat he did n' 'pear ter 'low he had ter do any co'tin', en w'en he 'd run 'cross Chloe 'bout de house, he 'd swell roun' 'er in a biggity way en say:—

"'Come heah en kiss me, honey. You gwine ter be mine in de spring. You doan 'pear ter be ez fon' er me ez you oughter be.'

"Chloe did n' keer nuffin fer Hannibal, en had n' keered nuffin fer 'im, en she sot des ez much sto' by Jeff ez she did de day she fus' laid eyes on 'im. En de mo' fermilyus dis yer Hannibal got, de mo' Chloe let her min' run on Jeff, en one ebenin' she went down ter de qua'ters en watch', 'tel she got a chance fer ter talk wid 'im by hisse'f. En she tol' Jeff fer ter go down en see ole Aun' Peggy, de cunjuh 'oman down by de Wim'l'ton Road, en ax her ter gib 'im sump'n ter he'p git Hannibal out'n de big house, so de w'ite folks u'd sen' fer Jeff ag'in. En bein' ez Jeff did n' hab nuffin ter gib Aun' Peggy, Chloe gun 'im a silber dollah en a silk han'kercher fer ter pay her wid, fer Aun' Peggy neber lack ter wuk fer nobody fer nuffin.

"So Jeff slip' off down ter Aun' Peggy's one night, en gun 'er de present he brung, en tol' 'er all 'bout 'im en Chloe en Hannibal, en ax' 'er ter he'p 'im out. Aun' Peggy tol' 'im she 'd wuk 'er roots, en fer 'im ter come back de nex' night, en she 'd tell 'im w'at she c'd do fer 'im.

"So de nex' night Jeff went back, en Aun' Peggy gun 'im a baby doll, wid a body made out'n a piece er co'n-stalk, en wid splinters fer a'ms en laigs, en a head made out'n elderberry peth, en two little red peppers fer feet.

"'Dis yer baby doll,' sez she, 'is Hannibal. Dis yer peth head is Hannibal's head, en dese yer pepper feet is Hannibal's feet. You take dis en hide it unner de house, on de sill unner de do', whar Hannibal 'll hafter walk ober it eve'y day. En ez long ez Hannibal comes anywhar nigh dis baby doll, he'll be des lack it is,—light-headed en hot-footed; en ef dem two things doan git 'im inter trouble mighty soon, den I'm no cunjuh 'oman. But w'en you git Hannibal out'n de house, en git all th'oo wid dis baby doll, you mus' fetch it back ter me, fer it's monst'us powerful goopher, en is liable ter make mo' trouble ef you leabe it layin' roun'.'

"Well, Jeff tuk de baby doll, en slip' up ter de big house, en whistle' ter Chloe, en w'en she come out he tol' 'er w'at ole Aun' Peggy had said. En Chloe showed 'im how ter git unner de house, en w'en he had put de cunjuh doll on de sill, he went 'long back ter de qua'ters—en des waited.

"Nex' day, sho' 'nuff, de goopher 'mence' ter wuk. Hannibal sta'ted in de house soon in de mawnin' wid a armful er wood ter make a fire, en he had n' mo' d'n got 'cross de do'-sill befo' his feet begun ter bu'n so dat he drap' de armful er wood on de flo' en woke ole mis' up a' hour sooner 'n yushal, en co'se ole mis' did n' lack dat, en spoke sha'p erbout it.

"W'en dinner-time come, en Hannibal wuz help'n' de cook kyar de dinner f'm de kitchen inter de big house, en wuz gittin' close ter de do' whar he had ter go in, his feet sta'ted ter bu'n en his head begun ter swim, en he let de big dish er chicken en dumplin's fall right down in de dirt, in de middle er de ya'd, en de w'ite folks had ter make dey dinner dat day off'n col' ham en sweet'n' 'taters.

"De nex' mawnin' he overslep' hisse'f, en got inter mo' trouble. Atter breakfus', Mars' Dugal' sont 'im ober ter Mars' Marrabo Utley's fer ter borry a monkey wrench. He oughter be'n back in ha'f a' hour, but he come pokin' home 'bout dinner-time wid a screw-driver stidder a monkey wrench. Mars' Dugal' sont ernudder nigger back wid de screw-driver, en Hannibal did n' git no dinner. 'Long in de afternoon, ole mis' sot Hannibal ter weedin' de flowers in de front gya'den, en Hannibal dug up all de bulbs ole mis' had sont erway fer, en paid a lot er money fer, en tuk 'em down ter de hawg-pen by de ba'nya'd, en fed 'em ter de hawgs. Wen ole mis' come out in de cool er de ebenin', en seed w'at Hannibal had done, she wuz mos' crazy, en she wrote a note en sont Hannibal down ter de oberseah wid it.

"But w'at Hannibal got fum de oberseah did n' 'pear ter do no good. Eve'y now en den 'is feet 'd 'mence ter torment 'im, en 'is min' 'u'd git all mix' up, en his conduc' kep' gittin' wusser en wusser, 'tel fin'lly de w'ite folks could n' stan' it no longer, en Mars' Dugal' tuk Hannibal back down ter de qua'ters.

"'Mr. Smif,' sez Mars' Dugal' ter de oberseah, 'dis yer nigger has done got so triflin' yer lately dat we can't keep 'im at de house no mo', en I 's fotch' 'im ter you ter be straighten' up. You 's had 'casion ter deal wid 'im once, so he knows w'at ter expec'. You des take 'im in han', en lemme know how he tu'ns out. En w'en de han's comes in fum de fiel' dis ebenin' you kin sen' dat yaller nigger Jeff up ter de house. I 'll try 'im, en see ef he's any better 'n Hannibal.'

"So Jeff went up ter de big house, en pleas' Mars' Dugal' en ole mis' en de res' er de fambly so well dat dey all got ter lackin' 'im fus'rate; en dey 'd 'a' fergot all 'bout Hannibal, ef it had n' be'n fer de bad repo'ts w'at come up fum de qua'ters 'bout 'im fer a mont' er so. Fac' is, dat Chloe en Jeff wuz so int'rusted in one ernudder sence Jeff be'n up ter de house, dat dey fergot all 'bout takin' de baby doll back ter Aun' Peggy, en it kep' wukkin' fer a w'ile, en makin' Hannibal's feet bu'n mo' er less, 'tel all de folks on de plantation got ter callin' 'im Hot-Foot Hannibal. He kep' gittin' mo' en mo' triflin', 'tel he got de name er bein' de mos' no 'countes' nigger on de plantation, en Mars' Dugal' had ter th'eaten ter sell 'im in de spring, w'en bimeby de goopher quit wukkin', en Hannibal 'mence' ter pick up some en make folks set a little mo' sto' by 'im.

"Now, dis yer Hannibal was a monst'us sma't nigger, en w'en he got rid er dem so' feet, his min' kep' runnin' on 'is udder troubles. Heah th'ee er fo' weeks befo' he 'd had a' easy job, waitin' on de w'ite folks, libbin' off'n de fat er de lan', en promus' de fines' gal on de plantation fer a wife in de spring, en now heah he wuz back in de co'n-fiel, wid de oberseah a-cussin' en a-r'arin' ef he did n' get a ha'd tas' done; wid nuffin but co'n bread en bacon en merlasses ter eat; en all de fiel'-han's makin' rema'ks, en pokin' fun at 'im 'ca'se he 'd be'n sont back fum de big house ter de fiel'. En de mo' Hannibal studied 'bout it de mo' madder he got, 'tel he fin'lly swo' he wuz gwine ter git eben wid Jeff en Chloe, ef it wuz de las' ac'.

"So Hannibal slipped 'way fum de qua'ters one Sunday en hid in de co'n up close ter de big house, 'tel he see Chloe gwine down de road. He waylaid her, en sezee:—

"'Hoddy, Chloe?'

"'I ain' got no time fer ter fool wid fiel'-han's,' sez Chloe, tossin' her head; 'w'at you want wid me, Hot-Foot?'

"'I wants ter know how you en Jeff is gittin' 'long.'

"'I 'lows dat's none er yo' bizness, nigger. I doan see w'at 'casion any common fiel'-han' has got ter mix in wid de 'fairs er folks w'at libs in de big house. But ef it'll do you any good ter know, I mought say dat me en Jeff is gittin' 'long mighty well, en we gwine ter git married in de spring, en you ain' gwine ter be 'vited ter de weddin' nuther.'

"'No, no!' sezee, 'I would n' 'spec' ter be 'vited ter de weddin',—a common, low-down fiel'-han' lack *I* is. But I's glad ter heah you en Jeff is gittin' 'long so well. I did n' knowed but w'at he had 'mence' ter be a little ti'ed.'

"'Ti'ed er me? Dat's rediklus!' sez Chloe. 'W'y, dat nigger lubs me so I b'liebe he 'd go th'oo fire en water fer me. Dat nigger is des wrop' up in me.'

"'Uh huh,' sez Hannibal, 'den I reckon it mus' be some udder nigger w'at meets a 'oman down by de crick in de swamp eve'y Sunday ebenin', ter say nuffin 'bout two er th'ee times a week.'

"'Yas, hit is ernudder nigger, en you is a liah w'en you say it wuz Jeff.'

"'Mebbe I is a liah, en mebbe I ain' got good eyes. But 'less'n I is a liah, en 'less'n I *ain'* got good eyes, Jeff is gwine ter meet dat 'oman dis ebenin' 'long 'bout eight o'clock right down dere by de crick in de swamp 'bout half-way betwix' dis plantation en Mars' Marrabo Utley's.'

"Well, Chloe tol' Hannibal she did n' b'liebe a wo'd he said, en call' 'im a low-down nigger, who wuz tryin' ter slander Jeff 'ca'se he wuz mo' luckier 'n he wuz. But all de same, she could n' keep her min' fum runnin' on w'at Hannibal had said. She 'membered she 'd heared one er de niggers say dey wuz a gal ober at Mars' Marrabo Utley's plantation w'at Jeff use' ter go wid some befo' he got 'quainted wid Chloe. Den she 'mence' ter figger back, en sho' 'nuff, dey wuz two er th'ee times in de las' week w'en she 'd be'n he'pin' de ladies wid dey dressin' en udder fixin's in de ebenin', en Jeff mought 'a' gone down ter de swamp widout her knowin' 'bout it at all. En den she 'mence' ter 'member little things w'at she had n' tuk no notice of befo', en w'at 'u'd make it 'pear lack Jeff had sump'n on his min'.

"Chloe set a monst'us heap er sto' by Jeff, en would 'a' done mos' anythin' fer 'im, so long ez he stuck ter her. But Chloe wuz a mighty jealous 'oman, en w'iles she didn' b'liebe w'at Hannibal said, she seed how it *could* 'a' be'n so, en she 'termine' fer ter fin' out fer herse'f whuther it *wuz* so er no.

"Now, Chloe had n' seed Jeff all day, fer Mars' Dugal' had sont Jeff ober ter his daughter's house, young Mis' Ma'g'ret's, w'at libbed 'bout fo' miles fum Mars' Dugal's, en Jeff wuz n' 'spected home 'tel ebenin'. But des atter supper wuz ober, en w'iles de ladies wuz settin' out on de piazzer, Chloe slip' off fum de house en run down de road,—dis yer same road we come; en w'en she got mos' ter de crick—dis yer same crick right befo' us—she kin' er kep' in de bushes at de side er de road, 'tel fin'lly she seed Jeff settin' on de bank on de udder side er de crick,— right unner dat ole wilier-tree droopin' ober de water yander. En eve'y now en den he 'd git up en look up de road to'ds Mars' Marrabo's on de udder side er de swamp.

"Fus' Chloe felt lack she 'd go right ober de crick en gib Jeff a piece er her min'. Den she 'lowed she better be sho' befo' she done anythin'. So she helt herse'f in de bes' she could, gittin' madder en madder eve'y minute, 'tel bimeby she seed a 'oman comin' down de road on de udder side fum to'ds Mars' Marrabo Utley's plantation. En w'en she seed Jeff jump up en run to'ds dat 'oman, en th'ow his a'ms roun' her neck, po' Chloe did n' stop ter see no mo', but des tu'nt roun' en run up ter de house, en rush' up on de piazzer, en up en tol' Mars' Dugal' en ole mis'

CHARLES W. CHESNUTT

all 'bout de baby doll, en all 'bout Jeff gittin' de goopher fum Aun' Peggy, en 'bout w'at de goopher had done ter Hannibal.

"Mars' Dugal' wuz monst'us mad. He did n' let on at fus' lack he b'liebed Chloe, but w'en she tuk en showed 'im whar ter fin' de baby doll, Mars' Dugal' tu'nt w'ite ez chalk.

"'Wat debil's wuk is dis?' sezee. 'No wonder de po' nigger's feet eetched. Sump'n got ter be done ter l'arn dat ole witch ter keep her han's off'n my niggers. En ez fer dis yer Jeff, I'm gwine ter do des w'at I promus', so de darkies on dis plantation'll know I means w'at I sez.'

"Fer Mars' Dugal' had warned de han's befo' 'bout foolin' wid cunju'ation; fac', he had los' one er two niggers his-se'f fum dey bein' goophered, en he would 'a' had ole Aun' Peggy whip' long ago, on'y Aun' Peggy wuz a free 'oman, en he wuz 'feard she 'd cunjuh him. En w'iles Mars' Dugal' say he did n' b'liebe in cunj'in' en sich, he 'peared ter 'low it wuz bes' ter be on de safe side, en let Aun' Peggy alone.

"So Mars' Dugal' done des ez he say. Ef ole mis' had ple'd fer Jeff, he mought 'a' kep' 'im. But ole mis' had n' got ober losin' dem bulbs yit, en she neber said a wo'd. Mars' Dugal' tuk Jeff ter town nex' day en' sol' 'im ter a spekilater, who sta'ted down de ribber wid 'im nex' mawnin' on a steamboat, fer ter take 'im ter Alabama.

"Now, w'en Chloe tol' ole Mars' Dugal' 'bout dis yer baby doll en dis udder goopher, she had n' ha'dly 'lowed Mars' Dugal' would sell Jeff down Souf. Howsomeber, she wuz so mad wid Jeff dat she 'suaded herse'f she did n' keer; en so she hilt her head up en went roun' lookin' lack she wuz rale glad 'bout it. But one day she wuz walkin' down de road, w'en who sh'd come 'long but dis yer Hannibal.

"W'en Hannibal seed 'er, he bus' out laffin' fittin' fer ter kill: 'Yah, yah, yah! ho, ho, ho! ha, ha, ha! Oh, hol' me, honey, hol' me, er I'll laf myse'f ter def. I ain' nebber laf' so much sence I be'n bawn.'

"'Wat you laffin' at, Hot-Foot?'

"'Yah, yah, yah! Wat I laffin' at? W'y, I's laffin' at myse'f, tooby sho',— laffin' ter think w'at a fine 'oman I made.'

"Chloe tu'nt pale, en her hea't come up in her mouf.

"'Wat you mean, nigger?' sez she, ketchin' holt er a bush by de road fer ter stiddy herse'f. 'Wat you mean by de kin' er 'oman you made?'

"'Wat do I mean? I means dat I got squared up wid you fer treatin' me de way you done, en I got eben wid dat yaller nigger Jeff fer cuttin' me out. Now, he's gwine ter know w'at it is ter cat co'n bread en merlasses once mo', en wuk fum daylight ter da'k, en ter hab a oberseah dribin' 'im fum one day's een' ter de udder. I means dat I sont wo'd ter Jeff dat Sunday dat you wuz gwine ter be ober ter Mars' Marrabo's visitin' dat ebenin', en you want 'im ter meet you down by de crick on de way home en go de rest er de road wid you. En den I put on a frock en a sunbonnet, en fix' myse'f up ter look lack a 'oman; en w'en Jeff seed me comin', he run ter meet me, en you seed 'im,—fer I'd be'n watchin' in de bushes befo' en 'skivered you comin' down de road. En now I reckon you en Jeff bofe knows w'at it means ter mess wid a nigger lack me.'

"Po' Chloe had n' heared mo' d'n half er de las' part er w'at Hannibal said, but she had heared 'nuff to l'arn dat dis nigger had fooled her en Jeff, en dat po' Jeff had n' done nuffin, en dat fer lovin' her too much en goin' ter meet her she had cause' 'im ter be sol' erway whar she'd neber, neber see 'im no mo'. De sun mought shine by day, de moon by night, de flowers mought bloom, en de mawkin'-birds mought sing, but po' Jeff wuz done los' ter her fereber en fereber.

"Hannibal had n' mo' d'n finish' w'at he had ter say, w'en Chloe's knees gun 'way unner her, en she fell down in de road, en lay dere half a' hour er so befo' she come to. W'en she did, she crep' up ter de house des ez pale ez a ghos'. En fer a mont' er so she crawled roun' de house, en 'peared ter be so po'ly dat Mars' Dugal' sont fer a doctor; en de doctor kep' on axin' her questions 'tel he foun' she wuz des pinin' erway fer Jeff.

"Wen he tol' Mars' Dugal', Mars' Dugal' lafft, en said he'd fix dat. She could hab de noo house boy fer a husban'. But ole mis' say, no, Chloe ain' dat kin'er gal, en dat Mars' Dugal' sh'd buy Jeff back.

"So Mars' Dugal' writ a letter ter dis yer spekilater down ter Wim'l'ton, en tol' ef he ain' done sol' dat nigger Souf w'at he bought fum 'im, he'd lack ter buy 'im back ag'in. Chloe 'mence' ter pick up a little w'en ole mis' tol' her 'bout dis letter. Howsomeber, bimeby Mars' Dugal' got a' answer fum de spekilater, who said he wuz monst'us sorry, but Jeff had fell ove'boa'd er jumped off'n de steamboat on de way ter Wim'l'ton, en got drownded, en co'se he could n' sell 'im back, much ez he'd lack ter 'bleedge Mars' Dugal'.

"Well, atter Chloe heared dis, she wa'n't much mo' use ter nobody. She pu'tended ter do her wuk, en ole mis' put up wid her, en had de doctor gib her medicine, en let 'er go ter de circus, en all so'ts er things fer ter take her min' off'n her troubles. But dey did n' none un 'em do no good. Chloe got ter slippin' down here in de ebenin' des lack she 'uz comin' ter meet Jeff, en she'd set dere unner dat wilier-tree on de udder side, en wait fer 'im, night atter night. Bimeby she got so bad de w'ite folks sont her ober ter young Mis' Ma'g'ret's fer ter gib her a change; but she runned erway de fus' night, en w'en dey looked fer 'er nex' mawnin', dey foun' her co'pse layin' in de branch yander, right 'cross fum whar we 're settin' now.

"Eber sence den," said Julius in conclusion, "Chloe's ha'nt comes eve'y ebenin' en sets down unner dat willer-tree en waits fer Jeff, er e'se walks up en down de road yander, lookin' en lookin', en waitin' en waitin', fer her sweethea't w'at ain' neber, neber come back ter her no mo'."

There was silence when the old man had finished, and I am sure I saw a tear in my wife's eye, and more than one in Mabel's.

"I think, Julius," said my wife, after a moment, "that you may turn the mare around and go by the long road."

The old man obeyed with alacrity, and I noticed no reluctance on the mare's part.

"You are not afraid of Chloe's haunt, are you?" I asked jocularly.

My mood was not responded to, and neither of the ladies smiled.

"Oh, no," said Annie, "but I've changed my mind. I prefer the other route."

When we had reached the main road and had proceeded along it for a short distance, we met a cart driven by a young negro, and on the cart were a trunk and a valise. We recognized the man as Malcolm Murchison's servant, and drew up a moment to speak to him.

"Who's going away, Marshall?" I inquired.

"Young Mistah Ma'colm gwine 'way on de boat ter Noo Yo'k dis ebenin', suh, en I'm takin' his things down ter de wharf, suh."

This was news to me, and I heard it with regret. My wife looked sorry, too, and I could see that Mabel was trying hard to hide her concern.

"He's comin' 'long behin', suh, en I 'spec's you'll meet 'im up de road a piece. He's gwine ter walk down ez fur ez Mistah Jim Williams's, en take de buggy fum dere ter town. He 'spec's ter be gone a long time, suh, en say prob'ly he ain' neber comin' back."

The man drove on. There were a few words exchanged in an undertone between my wife and Mabel, which I did not catch. Then Annie said: "Julius, you may stop the rockaway a moment. There are some trumpet-flowers by the road there that I want. Will you get them for me, John?"

I sprang into the underbrush, and soon returned with a great bunch of scarlet blossoms.

"Where is Mabel?" I asked, noting her absence.

"She has walked on ahead. We shall overtake her in a few minutes."

The carriage had gone only a short distance when my wife discovered that she had dropped her fan.

"I had it where we were stopping. Julius, will you go back and get it for me?"

Julius got down and went back for the fan. He was an unconscionably long time finding it. After we got started again we had gone only a little way, when we saw Mabel and young Murchison coming toward us. They were walking arm in arm, and their faces were aglow with the light of love.

I do not know whether or not Julius had a previous understanding with Malcolm Murchison by which he was to drive us round by the long road that day, nor do I know exactly what motive influenced the old man's exertions in the matter. He was fond of Mabel, but I was old enough, and knew Julius well enough, to be skeptical of his motives. It is certain that a most excellent understanding existed between him and Murchison after the reconciliation, and that when the young people set up housekeeping over at the old Murchison place, Julius had an opportunity to enter their service. For some reason or other, however, he preferred to remain with us. The mare, I might add, was never known to balk again.

# APPENDIX

Uncollected Uncle Julius Stories
    Dave's Neckliss (1889)
    A Deep Sleeper (1893)
    Lonesome Ben (1900)

Essay
    Superstitions and Folk-Lore of the South (1901)

# Dave's Neckliss

H ave some dinner, Uncle Julius?" said my wife. It was a Sunday afternoon in early autumn. Our two women-servants had gone to a camp-meeting some miles away, and would not return until evening. My wife had served the dinner, and we were just rising from the table, when Julius came up the lane, and, taking off his hat, seated himself on the piazza.

The old man glanced through the open door at the dinner-table, and his eyes rested lovingly upon a large sugar-cured ham, from which several slices had been cut, exposing a rich pink expanse that would have appealed strongly to the appetite of any hungry Christian.

"Thanky, Miss Annie," he said, after a momentary hesitation, "I dunno ez I keers ef I does tas'e a piece er dat ham, ef yer'll cut me off a slice un it."

"No," said Annie, "I won't. Just sit down to the table and help yourself; eat all you want, and don't be bashful."

Julius drew a chair up to the table, while my wife and I went out on the piazza. Julius was in my employment; he took his meals with his own family, but when he happened to be about our house at meal-times, my wife never let him go away hungry.

I threw myself into a hammock, from which I could see Julius through an open window. He ate with evident relish, devoting his attention chiefly to the ham, slice after slice of which disappeared in the spacious cavity of his mouth. At first the old man ate rapidly, but after the edge of his appetite had been taken off he proceeded in a more leisurely manner. When he had cut the sixth slice of ham (I kept count of them from a lazy curiosity to see how much he *could* eat) I saw him lay it on his plate; as he adjusted the knife and fork to cut it into smaller pieces, he paused, as if struck by a sudden thought, and a tear rolled down his rugged cheek and fell upon the slice of ham before him. But the emotion, whatever the thought that caused it, was transitory, and in a moment he continued his dinner. When he was through eating, he came out on the porch, and resumed his seat with the satisfied expression of countenance that usually follows a good dinner.

"Julius," I said, "you seemed to be affected by something, a moment ago. Was the mustard so strong that it moved you to tears?"

"No, suh, it wa'n't de mustard; I wuz studyin' 'bout Dave."

"Who was Dave, and what about him?" I asked.

The conditions were all favorable to story-telling. There was an autumnal languor in the air, and a dreamy haze softened the dark green of the distant pines and the deep blue of the Southern sky. The generous meal he had made had put the old man in a very good humor. He was not always so, for his curiously undeveloped nature was subject to moods which were almost childish in their variableness. It was only now and then that we were able to study, through the medium of his recollection, the simple but intensely human inner life of slavery. His way of looking at the past seemed very strange to us; his view of certain sides of life was essentially different from ours. He never indulged in any regrets for the Arcadian joyousness and irresponsibility which was a somewhat popular conception of slavery; his had not been the lot of the petted house-servant, but that of the toiling field-hand. While he mentioned with a warm appreciation the acts of kindness which those in authority had shown to him and his people, he would speak of a cruel deed, not with the indignation of one accustomed to quick feeling and spontaneous expression, but with a furtive disapproval which suggested to us a doubt in his own mind as to whether he had a right to think or to feel, and presented to us the curious psychological spectacle of a mind enslaved long after the shackles had been struck off from the limbs of its possessor. Whether the sacred name of liberty ever set his soul aglow with a generous fire; whether he had more than the most elementary ideas of love, friendship, patriotism, religion,—things which are half, and the better half, of life to us; whether he even realized, except in a vague, uncertain way, his own degradation, I do not know. I fear not; and if not, then centuries of repression had borne their legitimate fruit. But in the simple human feeling, and still more in the undertone of sadness, which pervaded his stories, I thought I could see a spark which, fanned by favoring breezes and fed by the memories of the past, might become in his children's children a glowing flame of sensibility, alive to every thrill of human happiness or human woe.

"Dave use' ter b'long ter my ole marster," said Julius; "he wuz raise' on dis yer plantation, en I kin 'member all erbout 'im, fer I wuz ole 'nuff ter chop cotton w'en it all happen'. Dave wuz a tall man, en monst'us strong: he could do mo' wuk in a day dan any yuther two niggers on de plantation. He wuz one er dese yer solemn kine er men, en nebber run on wid much foolishness, like de yuther darkies. He use' ter go out in de woods en pray; en w'en he hear de han's on de plantation cussin' en gwine on wid dere dancin' en foolishness, he use' ter tell 'em 'bout religion en jedgmen'-day, w'en dey would haf ter gin account fer eve'y idle word en all dey yuther sinful kyarin's-on.

"Dave had l'arn' how ter read de Bible. Dey wuz a free nigger boy in de settlement w'at wuz monst'us smart, en could write en cipher, en wuz alluz readin' books er papers. En Dave had hi'ed dis free boy fer ter l'arn 'im how ter read. Hit wuz 'g'in' de law, but co'se none er de niggers did n' say nuffin ter de w'ite folks 'bout it. Howsomedever, one day Mars Walker—he wuz de oberseah—foun' out Dave could read. Mars Walker wa'n't nuffin but a po' bockrah, en folks said he could n' read ner write hisse'f, en co'se he didn' lack ter see a nigger w'at knowed mo' d'n he did; so he went en tole Mars Dugal'. Mars Dugal' sont fer Dave, en ax' 'im 'bout it.

"Dave didn't hardly knowed w'at ter do; but he could n' tell no lie, so he 'fessed he could read de Bible a little by spellin' out de words. Mars Dugal' look' mighty solemn.

"'Dis yer is a se'ious matter,' sezee; 'it's 'g'in' de law ter l'arn niggers how ter read, er 'low 'em ter hab books. But w'at yer l'arn out'n dat Bible, Dave?'

"Dave wa'n't no fool, ef he wuz a nigger, en sezee:—

"'Marster, I l'arns dat it's a sin fer ter steal, er ter lie, er fer ter want w'at doan b'long ter yer; en I l'arns fer ter love de Lawd en ter 'bey my marster.'

"Mars Dugal' sorter smile' en laf ter hisse'f, like he 'uz might'ly tickle' 'bout sump'n, en sezee:—

"'Doan 'pear ter me lack readin' de Bible done yer much harm, Dave. Dat's w'at I wants all my niggers fer ter know. Yer keep right on readin', en tell de yuther han's w'at yer be'n tellin' me. How would yer lack fer ter preach ter de niggers on Sunday?'

"Dave say he 'd be glad fer ter do w'at he could. So Mars Dugal' tole de oberseah fer ter let Dave preach ter de niggers, en tell 'em w'at wuz in de Bible, en it would he'p ter keep 'em fum stealin' er runnin' erway.

"So Dave 'mence' ter preach, en done de han's on de plantation a heap er good, en most un 'em lef' off dey wicked ways, en 'mence' ter love ter hear 'bout God, en religion, en de Bible; en dey done dey wuk better, en didn' gib de oberseah but mighty little trouble fer ter manage 'em.

"Dave wuz one er dese yer men w'at did n' keer much fer de gals,—leastways he did n' 'tel Dilsey come ter de plantation. Dilsey wuz a monst'us peart, good-lookin', gingybread-colored gal,—one er dese yer high-steppin' gals w'at hol's dey heads up, en won' stan' no foolishness fum no man. She had b'long' ter a gemman over on Rockfish, w'at died, en whose 'state ha' ter be sol' fer ter pay his debts. En Mars Dugal' had be'n ter de oction, en w'en he seed dis gal a-cryin' en gwine on 'bout bein' sol' erway fum her ole mammy, Aun' Mahaly, Mars Dugal' bid 'em bofe in, en fotch 'em ober ter our plantation.

"De young nigger men on de plantation wuz des wil' atter Dilsey, but it did n' do no good, en none un 'em could n' git Dilsey fer dey junesey,* 'tel Dave 'mence' fer ter go roun' Aun' Mahaly's cabin. Dey wuz a fine-lookin' couple, Dave en Dilsey wuz, bofe tall, en well-shape', en soopl'. En dey sot a heap by one ernudder. Mars Dugal' seed 'em tergedder one Sunday, en de nex' time he seed Dave atter dat, sezee:—

"'Dave, w'en yer en Dilsey gits ready fer ter git married, I ain' got no rejections. Dey's a poun' er so er chawin'-terbacker up at de house, en I reckon yo' mist'iss kin fine a frock en a ribbin er two fer Dilsey. Youer bofe good niggers, en yer neenter be feared er bein' sol' 'way fum one ernudder long ez I owns dis plantation; en I 'spec's ter own it fer a long time yit.'

"But dere wuz one man on de plantation w'at did n' lack ter see Dave en Dilsey tergedder ez much ez ole marster did. W'en Mars Dugal' went ter de sale whar he got Dilsey en Mahaly, he bought ernudder ban', by de name er Wiley. Wiley wuz one er dese yer shiny-eyed, double-headed little niggers, sha'p ez a steel trap, en sly ez de fox w'at keep out'n it. Dis yer Wiley had be'n pesterin' Dilsey 'fo' she come ter our plantation, en had nigh 'bout worried de life out'n her. She did n' keer nuffin fer 'im, but he pestered her so she ha' ter th'eaten ter tell her marster fer ter make Wiley let her 'lone. W'en he come ober to our place it wuz des ez bad, 'tel bimeby Wiley seed dat Dilsey had got ter thinkin' a heap 'bout Dave, en den he sorter hilt off aw'ile, en purten' lack he gin Dilsey up. But he wuz one er dese yer 'ceitful niggers, en w'ile he wuz laffin' en jokin' wid de yuther ban's 'bout Dave en Dilsey, he wuz settin' a trap fer ter ketch Dave en git Dilsey back fer hisse'f.

"Dave en Dilsey made up dere min's fer ter git married long 'bout Christmas time, w'en dey 'd hab mo' time fer a weddin'. But 'long 'bout two weeks befo' dat time ole mars 'mence' ter lose a heap er bacon. Eve'y night er so somebody 'ud steal a side er bacon, er a ham, er a shoulder,

---

* Sweetheart.

　　　　　CHARLES W. CHESNUTT

er sump'n, fum one er de smoke-'ouses. De smoke-'ouses wuz lock', but somebody had a key, en manage' ter git in some way er 'nudder. Dey 's mo' ways 'n one ter skin a cat, en dey's mo' d'n one way ter git in a smoke-'ouse,—leastways dat's w'at I hearn say. Folks w'at had bacon fer ter sell did n' hab no trouble 'bout gittin' rid un it. Hit wuz 'g'in' de law fer ter buy things fum slabes; but Lawd! dat law did n' 'mount ter a hill er peas. Eve'y week er so one er dese yer big covered waggins would come 'long de road, peddlin' terbacker en w'iskey. Dey wuz a sight er room in one er dem big waggins, en it wuz monst'us easy fer ter swop off bacon fer sump'n ter chaw er ter wa'm yer up in de wintertime. I s'pose de peddlers did n' knowed dey wuz breakin' de law, caze de niggers alluz went at night, en stayed on de dark side er de waggin; en it wuz mighty hard fer ter tell *w'at* kine er folks dey wuz.

"Atter two er th'ee hund'ed er meat had be'n stole', Mars Walker call all de niggers up one ebenin', en tol' 'em dat de fus' nigger he cot stealin' bacon on dat plantation would git sump'n fer ter 'member it by long ez he lib'. En he say he'd gin fi' dollars ter de nigger w'at 'skiver' de rogue. Mars Walker say he s'picion' one er two er de niggers, but he could n' tell fer sho, en co'se dey all 'nied it w'en he 'cuse em un it.

"Dey wa'n't no bacon stole' fer a week er so, 'tel one dark night w'en somebody tuk a ham fum one er de smoke-'ouses. Mars Walker des cusst awful w'en he foun' out de ham wuz gone, en say he gwine ter sarch all de niggers' cabins; w'en dis yer Wiley I wuz tellin' yer 'bout up'n say he s'picion' who tuk de ham, fer he seed Dave comin' 'cross de plantation fum to'ds de smoke-'ouse de night befo'. W'en Mars Walker hearn dis fum Wiley, he went en sarch' Dave's cabin, en foun' de ham hid under de flo'.

"Eve'ybody wuz 'stonish'; but dere wuz de ham. Co'se Dave 'nied it ter de las', but dere wuz de ham. Mars Walker say it wuz des ez he 'spected: he did n' b'lieve in dese yer readin' en prayin' niggers; it wuz all 'pocrisy, en sarve' Mars Dugal' right fer 'lowin' Dave ter be readin' books w'en it wuz 'g'in' de law.

"W'en Mars Dugal hearn 'bout de ham, he say he wuz might'ly 'ceived en disapp'inted in Dave. He say he wouldn' nebber hab no mo' conference in no nigger, en Mars Walker could do des ez he wuz a mineter wid Dave er any er de res' er de niggers. So Mars Walker tuk'n tied Dave up en gin 'im forty; en den he got some er dis yer wire clof w'at dey uses fer ter make sifters out'n, en tuk'n wrap' it roun' de ham en fasten it tergedder at de little een'. Den he tuk Dave down ter de blacksmif-shop, en had Unker Silas, de plantation blacksmif, fasten a chain ter de ham, en den fasten de yuther een' er de chain roun' Dave's neck. En den he says ter Dave, sezee:—

"'Now, suh, yer'll wear dat neckliss fer de nex' six mont's; en I 'spec's yer ner none er de yuther niggers on dis plantation won' steal no mo' bacon dyoin' er dat time.'

"Well, it des 'peared ez if fum dat time Dave did n' hab nuffin but trouble. De niggers all turnt ag'in' 'im, caze he be'n de 'casion er Mars Dugal' turnin' 'em all ober ter Mars Walker. Mars Dugal' wa'n't a bad marster hisse'f, but Mars Walker wuz hard ez a rock. Dave kep' on sayin' he did n' take de ham, but none un 'em did n' b'lieve 'im.

"Dilsey wa'n't on de plantation w'en Dave wuz 'cused er stealin' de bacon. Ole mist'iss had sont her ter town fer a week er so fer ter wait on one er her darters w'at had a young baby, en she didn' fine out nuffin 'bout Dave's trouble 'tel she got back ter de plantation. Dave had patien'ly endyoed de finger er scawn, en all de hard words w'at de niggers pile' on 'im, caze he wuz sho' Dilsey would stan' by 'im, en would n' b'lieve he wuz a rogue, ner none er de yuther tales de darkies wuz tellin' 'bout 'im.

"W'en Dilsey come back fum town, en got down fum behine de buggy whar she b'en ridin' wid ole mars, de fus' nigger 'ooman she met says ter her,—

"'Is yer seed Dave, Dilsey?'

"'No, I ain' seed Dave,' says Dilsey.

"'Yer des oughter look at dat nigger; reckon yer would n' want 'im fer yo' junesey no mo'. Mars Walker cotch 'im stealin' bacon, en gone en fasten' a ham roun' his neck, so he can't git it off'n hisse'f. He sut'nly do look quare.' En den de 'ooman bus' out laffin' fit ter kill herse'f. W'en she got thoo laffin' she up'n tole Dilsey all 'bout de ham, en all de yuther lies w'at de niggers be'n tellin' on Dave.

"W'en Dilsey started down ter de quarters, who should she meet but Dave, comin' in fum de cotton-fiel'. She turnt her head ter one side, en purten' lack she did n' seed Dave.

"'Dilsey!' sezee.

"Dilsey walk' right on, en did n' notice 'im.

"'*Oh*, Dilsey!'

"Dilsey did n' paid no 'tention ter 'im, en den Dave knowed some er de niggers be'n tellin' her 'bout de ham. He felt monst'us bad, but he 'lowed ef he could des git Dilsey fer ter listen ter 'im fer a minute er so, he could make her b'lieve he did n' stole de bacon. It wuz a week er two befo' he could git a chance ter speak ter her ag'in; but fine'ly he cotch her down by de spring one day, en sezee:—

"'Dilsey, w'at fer yer won' speak ter me, en purten' lack yer doan see me? Dilsey, yer knows me too well fer ter b'lieve I 'd steal, er do dis yuther wick'ness de niggers is all layin' ter me,—yer *knows* I would n' do dat, Dilsey. Yer ain' gwine back on yo' Dave, is yer?'

"But w'at Dave say didn' hab no 'fec' on Dilsey. Dem lies folks b'en tellin' her had p'isen' her min' 'g'in' Dave.

"'I doan wanter talk ter no nigger,' says she, 'w'at be'n whip' fer stealin', en w'at gwine roun' wid sich a lookin' thing ez dat hung roun' his neck. I's a 'spectable gal, *I* is. W'at yer call dat, Dave? Is dat a cha'm fer ter keep off witches, er is it a noo kine er neckliss yer got?'

"Po' Dave did n' knowed w'at ter do. De las' one he had pended on fer ter stan' by 'im had gone back on 'im, en dey did n' 'pear ter be nuffin mo' wuf libbin' fer. He could n' hol' no mo' pra'r-meetin's, fer Mars Walker would n' 'low 'im ter preach, en de darkies would n' 'a' listen' ter 'im ef he had preach'. He didn' eben hab his Bible fer ter comfort hisse'f wid, fer Mars Walker had tuk it erway fum 'im en burnt it up, en say ef he ketch any mo' niggers wid Bibles on de plantation he 'd do 'em wuss'n he done Dave.

"En ter make it still harder fer Dave, Dilsey tuk up wid Wiley. Dave could see him gwine up ter Aun' Mahaly's cabin, en settin' out on de bench in de moonlight wid Dilsey, en singin' sinful songs en playin' de banjer. Dave use' ter scrouch down behine de bushes, en wonder w'at de Lawd sen' 'im all dem tribberlations fer.

"But all er Dave's yuther troubles wa'n't nuffin side er dat ham. He had wrap' de chain roun' wid a rag, so it did n' hurt his neck; but w'eneber he went ter wuk, dat ham would be in his way; he had ter do his task, howsomedever, des de same ez ef he did n' hab de ham. W'eneber he went ter lay down, dat ham would be in de way. Ef he turn ober in his sleep, dat ham would be tuggin' at his neck. It wuz de las' thing he seed at night, en de fus' thing he seed in de mawnin'. W'eneber he met a stranger, de ham would be de fus' thing de stranger would see. Most un 'em would 'mence' ter laf, en whareber Dave went he could see folks p'intin' at him, en year 'em sayin':—

"'W'at kine er collar dat nigger got roun' his neck?' er, ef dey knowed 'im, 'Is yer stole any mo' hams lately?' er 'W'at yer take fer yo' neckliss, Dave?' er some joke er 'nuther 'bout dat ham.

"Fus' Dave did n' mine it so much, caze he knowed he had n' done nuffin. But bimeby he got so he could n' stan' it no longer, en he 'd hide hisse'f in de bushes w'eneber he seed anybody comin', en alluz kep' hisse'f shet up in his cabin atter he come in fum wuk.

"It wuz monst'us hard on Dave, en bimeby, w'at wid dat ham eberlastin' en etarnally draggin' roun' his neck, he 'mence' fer ter do en say quare things, en make de niggers wonder ef he wa'n't gittin' out'n his mine. He got ter gwine roun' talkin' ter hisse'f, en singin' corn-shuckin' songs, en laffin' fit ter kill 'bout nuffin. En one day he tole one er de niggers he had 'skivered a noo way fer ter raise hams,—gwine ter pick 'em off'n trees, en save de expense er smoke-'ouses by kyoin' 'em in de sun. En one day he up'n tole Mars Walker he got sump'n pertickler fer ter say ter 'im; en he tuk Mars Walker off ter one side, en tole 'im he wuz gwine ter show 'im a place in de swamp whar dey wuz a whole trac' er lan' covered wid ham-trees.

"Wen Mars Walker hearn Dave talkin' dis kine er fool-talk, en w'en he seed how Dave wuz 'mencin' ter git behine in his wuk, en w'en he ax' de niggers en dey tole 'im how Dave be'n gwine on, he 'lowed he reckon' he 'd punish' Dave ernuff, en it mou't do mo' harm dan good fer ter keep de ham on his neck any longer. So he sont Dave down ter de blacksmif-shop en had de ham tuk off. Dey wa'n't much er de ham lef' by dat time, fer de sun had melt all de fat, en de lean had all swivel' up, so dey wa'n't but th'ee er fo' poun's lef'.

"W'en de ham had be'n tuk off'n Dave, folks kinder stopped talkin' 'bout 'im so much. But de ham had be'n on his neck so long dat Dave had sorter got use' ter it. He look des lack he 'd los' sump'n fer a day er so atter de ham wuz tuk off, en didn' 'pear ter know w'at ter do wid hisse'f; en fine'ly he up'n tuk'n tied a lighterd-knot ter a string, en hid it under de flo' er his cabin, en w'en nobody wuz n' lookin' he 'd take it out en hang it roun' his neck, en go off in de woods en holler en sing; en he allus tied it roun' his neck w'en he went ter sleep. Fac', it 'peared lack Dave done gone clean out'n his mine. En atter a w'ile he got one er de quarest notions you eber hearn tell un. It wuz 'bout dat time dat I come back ter de plantation fer ter wuk,—I had be'n out ter Mars Dugal's yuther place on Beaver Crick for a mont' er so. I had hearn 'bout Dave en de bacon, en 'bout w'at wuz gwine on on de plantation; but I did n' b'lieve w'at dey all say 'bout Dave, fer I knowed Dave wa'n't dat kine er man. One day atter I come back, me'n Dave wuz choppin' cotton tergedder, w'en Dave lean' on his hoe, en motion'

CHARLES W. CHESNUTT

fer me ter come ober close ter 'im; en den he retch' ober en w'ispered ter me.

"'Julius', sezee, 'did yer knowed yer wuz wukkin' long yer wid a ham?'

"I could n' 'magine w'at he meant. 'G'way fum yer, Dave,' says I. 'Yer ain' wearin' no ham no mo'; try en fergit 'bout dat; 't ain' gwine ter do yer no good fer ter 'member it.'

"'Look a-yer, Julius,' sezee, 'kin yer keep a secret?'

"'Co'se I kin, Dave,' says I. 'I doan go roun' tellin' people w'at yuther folks says ter me.'

"'Kin I trus' yer, Julius? Will yer cross yo' heart?'

"I cross' my heart. 'Wush I may die ef I tells a soul,' says I.

"Dave look' at me des lack he wuz lookin' thoo me en 'way on de yuther side er me, en sezee:—

"'Did yer knowed I wuz turnin' ter a ham, Julius?'

"I tried ter 'suade Dave dat dat wuz all foolishness, en dat he oughtn't ter be talkin' dat-a-way,—hit wa'n't right. En I tole 'im ef he 'd des be patien', de time would sho'ly come w'en eve'ything would be straighten' out, en folks would fine out who de rale rogue wuz w'at stole de bacon. Dave 'peared ter listen ter w'at I say, en promise' ter do better, en stop gwine on dat-a-way; en it seem lack he pick' up a bit w'en he seed dey wuz one pusson did n' b'lieve dem tales 'bout 'im.

"Hit wa'n't long atter dat befo' Mars Archie McIntyre, ober on de Wimbleton road, 'mence' ter complain 'bout somebody stealin' chickens fum his hen-'ouse. De chickens kep' on gwine, en at las' Mars Archie tole de ban's on his plantation dat he gwine ter shoot de fus' man he ketch in his hen-'ouse. In less'n a week atter he gin dis warnin', he cotch a nigger in de hen-'ouse, en fill' 'im full er squir'l-shot. W'en he got a light, he 'skivered it wuz a strange nigger; en w'en he call' one er his own sarven's, de nigger tole 'im it wuz our Wiley. W'en Mars Archie foun' dat out, he sont ober ter our plantation fer ter tell Mars Dugal' he had shot one er his niggers, en dat he could sen' ober dere en git w'at wuz lef un 'im.

"Mars Dugal' wuz mad at fus'; but w'en he got ober dere en hearn how it all happen', he did n' hab much ter say. Wiley wuz shot so bad he wuz sho' he wuz gwine ter die, so he up'n says ter ole marster:—

"'Mars Dugal',' sezee, 'I knows I's be'n a monst'us bad nigger, but befo' I go I wanter git sump'n off'n my mine. Dave didn' steal dat bacon w'at wuz tuk out'n de smoke-'ouse. I stole it all, en I hid de ham under Dave's cabin fer ter th'ow de blame on him—en may de good Lawd fergib me fer it.'

"Mars Dugal' had Wiley tuk back ter de plantation, en sont fer a doctor fer ter pick de shot out'n 'im. En de ve'y nex' mawnin' Mars Dugal' sont fer Dave ter come up ter de big house; he felt kinder sorry fer de way Dave had be'n treated. Co'se it wa'n't no fault er Mars Dugal's, but he wuz gwine ter do w'at he could fer ter make up fer it. So he sont word down ter de quarters fer Dave en all de yuther han's ter 'semble up in de yard befo' de big house at sun-up nex' mawnin'.

"Yearly in de mawnin' de niggers all swarm' up in de yard. Mars Dugal' wuz feelin' so kine dat he had brung up a bairl er cider, en tole de niggers all fer ter he'p deyselves.

"All de han's on de plantation come but Dave; en bimeby, w'en it seem lack he wa'n't comin', Mars Dugal' sont a nigger down ter de quarters ter look fer 'im. De sun wuz gittin' up, en dey wuz a heap er wuk ter be done, en Mars Dugal' sorter got ti'ed waitin'; so he up'n says:—

"'Well, boys en gals, I sont fer yer all up yer fer ter tell yer dat all dat 'bout Dave's stealin' er de bacon wuz a mistake, ez I s'pose yer all done hearn befo' now, en I 's mighty sorry it happen'. I wants ter treat all my niggers right, en I wants yer all ter know dat I sets a heap by all er my han's w'at is hones' en smart. En I want yer all ter treat Dave des lack yer did befo' dis thing happen', en mine w'at he preach ter yer; fer Dave is a good nigger, en has had a hard row ter hoe. En de fus' one I ketch sayin' anythin' 'g'in' Dave, I'll tell Mister Walker ter gin 'im forty. Now take ernudder drink er cider all roun', en den git at dat cotton, fer I wanter git dat Persimmon Hill trac' all pick' ober ter-day.'

"W'en de niggers wuz gwine 'way, Mars Dugal' tole me fer ter go en hunt up Dave, en bring 'im up ter de house. I went down ter Dave's cabin, but could n' fine 'im dere. Den I look' roun' de plantation, en in de aidge er de woods, en 'long de road; but I could n' fine no sign er Dave. I wuz 'bout ter gin up de sarch, w'en I happen' fer ter run 'cross a foot-track w'at look' lack Dave's. I had wukked 'long wid Dave so much dat I knowed his tracks: he had a monst'us long foot, wid a holler instep, w'ich wuz sump'n skase 'mongs' black folks. So I follered dat track 'cross de fiel' fum de quarters 'tel I got ter de smoke-'ouse. De fus' thing I notice' wuz smoke comin' out'n de cracks; it wuz cu'ous, caze dey had n' be'n no hogs kill' on de plantation fer six mont' er so, en all de bacon in de smoke-'ouse wuz done kyoed. I could n' 'magine fer ter sabe my life w'at Dave wuz doin' in dat smoke-'ouse. I went up ter de do' en hollered:—

"'Dave!'

CHARLES W. CHESNUTT

"Dey didn' nobody answer. I didn' wanter open de do', fer w'ite folks is monst'us pertickler 'bout dey smoke-'ouses; en ef de oberseah had a-come up en cotch me in dere, he mou't not wanter b'lieve I wuz des lookin' fer Dave. So I sorter knock at de do' en call' out ag'in:—

"'O Dave, hit's me—Julius! Doan be skeered. Mars Dugal' wants yer ter come up ter de big house,—he done 'skivered who stole de ham.'

"But Dave didn' answer. En w'en I look' roun' ag'in en didn' seed none er his tracks gwine way fum de smoke-'ouse, I knowed he wuz in dere yit, en I wuz 'termine' fer ter fetch 'im out; so I push de do' open en look in.

"Dey wuz a pile er bark burnin' in de middle er de flo', en right ober de fier, hangin' fum one er de rafters, wuz Dave; dey wuz a rope roun' his neck, en I didn' haf ter look at his face mo' d'n once fer ter see he wuz dead.

"Den I knowed how it all happen'. Dave had kep' on gittin' wusser en wusser in his mine, 'tel he des got ter b'lievin' he wuz all done turnt ter a ham; en den he had gone en built a fier, en tied a rope roun' his neck, des lack de hams wuz tied, en had hung hisse'f up in de smoke-'ouse fer ter kyo.

"Dave wuz buried down by de swamp, in de plantation buryin' groun'. Wiley didn' died fum de woun' he got in Mars McIntyre's hen 'ouse; he got well atter a w'ile, but Dilsey wouldn' hab nuffin mo' ter do wid 'im, en 't wa'n't long 'fo' Mars Dugal' sol' 'im ter a spekilater on his way souf,—he say he didn' want no sich a nigger on de plantation, ner in de county, ef he could he'p it. En w'en de een' er de year come, Mars Dugal" turnt Mars Walker off, en run de plantation hisse'f atter dat.

"Eber sence den," said Julius in conclusion, "w'eneber I eats ham, it min's me er Dave. I lacks ham, but I nebber kin eat mo' d'n two er th'ee poun's befo' I gits ter studyin' 'bout Dave, en den I has ter stop en leab de res' fer ernudder time."

There was a short silence after the old man had finished his story, and then my wife began to talk to him about the weather, on which subject he was an authority. I went into the house. When I came out, half an hour later, I saw Julius disappearing down the lane, with a basket on his arm.

At breakfast, next morning, it occurred to me that I should like a slice of ham. I said as much to my wife.

"Oh, no, John," she responded, "you shouldn't eat anything so heavy for breakfast."

I insisted.

"The fact is," she said, pensively, "I couldn't have eaten any more of that ham, and so I gave it to Julius."

# A Deep Sleeper

It was four o'clock on Sunday afternoon, in the month of July. The air had been hot and sultry, but a light, cool breeze had sprung up, and occasional cirrus clouds overspread the sun, and for a while subdued his fierceness. We were all out on the piazza—as the coolest place we could find—my wife, my sister-in-law and I. The only sounds that broke the Sabbath stillness were the hum of an occasional vagrant bumble-bee, or the fragmentary song of a mocking-bird in a neighboring elm, who lazily trolled a stave of melody, now and then, as a sample of what he could do in the cool of the morning, or after a light shower, when the conditions would be favorable to exertion.

"Annie," said I, "suppose, to relieve the deadly dulness of the afternoon, that we go out and pull the big watermelon, and send for Colonel Pemberton's folks to come over and help us eat it."

"Is it ripe, yet?" she inquired sleepily, brushing away a troublesome fly that had impudently settled on her hair.

"Yes, I think so. I was out yesterday with Julius, and we thumped it, and concluded it would be fully ripe by tomorrow or next day. But I think it is perfectly safe to pull it to-day."

"Well, if you are sure, dear, we'll go. But how can we get it up to the house? It's too big to tote."

"I'll step round to Julius's cabin and ask him to go down with the wheelbarrow and bring it up," I replied.

Julius was an elderly colored man who worked on the plantation and lived in a small house on the place, a few rods from my own residence. His daughter was our cook, and other members of his family served us in different capacities.

As I turned the corner of the house I saw Julius coming up the lane. He had on his Sunday clothes, and was probably returning from the afternoon meeting at the Sandy Run Baptist Church, of which he was a leading member and deacon.

"Julius," I said, "we are going out to pull the big watermelon, and we want you to take the wheelbarrow and go with us, and bring it up to the house."

"Does yer reckon dat watermillun's ripe yit, sah?" said Julius. "Didn' 'pear ter me it went quite plunk enuff yistiddy fer ter be pull' befo' termorrer."

"I think it is ripe enough, Julius."

"Mawnin' 'ud be a better time fer ter pull it, sah, w'en de night air an' de jew's done cool' it off nice."

"Probably that's true enough, but we'll put it on ice, and that will cool it; and I'm afraid if we leave it too long, some one will steal it."

"I 'spec's dat so," said the old man, with a confirmatory shake of the head. "Yer takes chances w'en yer pulls it, en' yer takes chances w'en yer don't. Dey's a lot er po' w'ite trash roun' heah w'at ain' none too good fer ter steal it. I seed some un' 'em loafin' long de big road on mer way home fum chu'ch jes' now. I has ter watch mer own chicken-coop ter keep chick'ns 'nuff fer Sunday eatin'. I'll go en' git de w'eelborrow."

Julius had a profound contempt for poor whites, and never let slip an opportunity for expressing it. He assumed that we shared this sentiment, while in fact our feeling toward this listless race was something entirely different. They were, like Julius himself, the product of a system which they had not created and which they did not know enough to resist.

As the old man turned to go away he began to limp, and put his hand to his knee with an exclamation of pain.

"What's the matter, Julius?" asked my wife.

"Yes, Uncle Julius, what ails you?" echoed her sweet young sister. "Did you stump your toe?"

"No, miss, it's dat mis'able rheumatiz. It ketches me now an' den in de lef' knee, so I can't hardly draw my bref. O Lawdy!" he added between his clenched teeth, "but dat do hurt. Ouch! It's a little better now," he said, after a moment, "but I doan' b'lieve I kin roll dat w'eelborrow out ter de watermillun-patch en' back. Ef it's all de same ter yo', sah, I'll go roun' ter my house en' sen' Tom ter take my place, w'iles I rubs some linimum on my laig."

"That'll be all right, Julius," I said, and the old man, hobbling, disappeared round the corner of the house. Tom was a lubberly, sleepy-looking negro boy of about fifteen, related to Julius's wife in some degree, and living with them.

The old man came back in about five minutes. He walked slowly, and seemed very careful about bearing his weight on the afflicted member.

"I sont 'Liza Jane fer ter wake Tom up," he said. "He's down in de orchard asleep under a tree somewhar. 'Liza Jane knows whar he is. It takes a minute er so fer ter wake 'im up. 'Liza Jane knows how ter do it. She tickles 'im in de nose er de yeah wid a broomstraw; hollerin' doan' do no good. Dat boy is one er de Seben Sleepers. He's wuss'n his gran'daddy used ter be."

"Was his grandfather a deep sleeper, Uncle Julius?" asked my wife's sister.

"Oh, yas, Miss Mabel," said Julius, gravely. "He wuz a monst'us pow'ful sleeper. He slep' fer a mont' once."

"Dear me, Uncle Julius, you must be joking," said my sister-in-law incredulously. I thought she put it mildly.

"Oh, no, ma'm, I ain't jokin'. I never jokes on ser'ous subjec's. I wuz dere w'en it all happen'. Hit wuz a monst'us quare thing."

"Sit down, Uncle Julius, and tell us about it," said Mabel; for she dearly loved a story, and spent much of her time "drawing out" the colored people in the neighborhood.

The old man took off his hat and seated himself on the top step of the piazza. His movements were somewhat stiff and he was very careful to get his left leg in a comfortable position.

"Tom's gran'daddy wuz name' Skundus," he began. "He had a brudder name' Tushus en' ernudder name' Cottus en' ernudder name' Squinchus." The old man paused a moment and gave his leg another hitch.

My sister-in-law was shaking with laughter. "What remarkable names!" she exclaimed. "Where in the world did they get them?"

"Dem names wuz gun ter 'em by ole Marse Dugal' McAdoo, wat I use' ter b'long ter, en' dey use' ter b'long ter. Marse Dugal' named all de babies w'at wuz bawn on de plantation. Dese young un's mammy wanted ter call 'em sump'n plain en' simple, like 'Rastus' er 'Cæsar' er 'George Wash'n'ton;' but ole Marse say no, he want all de niggers on his place ter hab diffe'nt names, so he kin tell 'em apart. He'd done use' up all de common names, so he had ter take sump'n else. Dem names he gun Skundus en' his brudders is Hebrew names en' wuz tuk out'n de Bible."

"Can you give me chapter and verse?" asked Mabel.

"No, Miss Mabel, I doan know 'em. Hit ain' my fault dat I ain't able ter read de Bible. But ez I wuz a-sayin', dis yer Skundus growed up ter be a peart, lively kind er boy, en' wuz very well liked on de plantation. He never quo'lled wid de res' er de ban's en' alluz behaved 'isse'f en' tended ter his wuk. De only fault he had wuz his sleep'ness. He'd haf ter be woke up ev'y mawnin' ter go ter his wuk, en' w'enever he got a chance he'd fall ersleep. He wuz might'ly nigh gittin' inter trouble mod'n once fer gwine ter sleep in de fiel'. I never seed his beat fer sleepin'. He could sleep in de sun er sleep in de shade. He could lean upon his hoe en' sleep. He went ter sleep walk'n' 'long de road oncet, en' mighty nigh bus't his head open 'gin' a tree he run inter. I did heah he oncet went ter sleep while he wuz in swimmin'. He wuz floatin' at de time, en' come mighty nigh gittin' drownded befo' he woke up. Ole Marse heared 'bout it en' ferbid his gwine in swimmin' enny mo', fer he said he couldn't 'ford ter lose 'im.

"When Skundus wuz growed up he got ter lookin' roun' at de gals, en' one er de likeliest un 'em tuk his eye. It was a gal name' Cindy, w'at libbed wid 'er mammy in a cabin by deyse'ves. Cindy tuk ter Skundus ez much ez Skundus tuk ter Cindy, en' bimeby Skundus axed his marster ef he could marry Cindy. Marse Dugal' b'long' ter de P'isbytay'n Chu'ch en' never 'lowed his niggers ter jump de broomstick, but alluz had a preacher fer ter marry 'em. So he tole Skundus ef him en' Cindy would 'ten' ter dey wuk good dat summer till de crap was laid by, he'd let 'em git married en' hab a weddin' down ter de quarters.

"So Skundus en' Cindy wukked hahd as dey could till 'bout a mont' er so befo' layin' by, w'en Marse Dugal's brudder, Kunnel Wash'n'ton McAdoo, w'at libbed down in Sampson County, 'bout a hunderd mile erway, come fer ter visit Marse Dugal'. Dey wuz five er six folks in de visitin' party, en' our w'ite folks needed a new gal fer ter he'p wait on 'em. Dey picked out de likeliest gal dey could fine 'mongs' de fiel-han's, en' 'cose dat wuz Cindy. Cindy wuz might'ly tickled fer ter be tuk in de house-sarvice, fer it meant better vittles en' better clo's en' easy wuk. She didn' seed Skundus quite as much, but she seed 'im w'eneber she could. Prospe'ity didn' spile Cindy; she didn' git stuck up en' 'bove 'sociatin' wid fiel'han's, lack some gals in her place 'ud a done.

"Cindy wuz sech a handy gal 'roun' de house, en' her marster's relations lacked her so much, dat w'en dey visit wuz ober, dey wanted ter take Cindy 'way wid 'em. Cindy didn' want ter go en' said so. Her marster wuz a good-natured kind er man, en' would 'a' kep' her on de plantation. But his wife say no, it 'ud nebber do ter be lett'n' de sarvants hab dey own way, er dey soon wouldn' be no doin' nuthin' wid 'em. Ole marster tole 'er he done promus ter let Cindy marry Skundus.

"'O, well,' sez ole Miss, 'dat doan' cut no figger. Dey's too much er dis foolishness 'bout husban's en' wibes 'mongs' de niggers now-a-days. One nigger man is de same as ernudder, en' dey'll be plenty un 'em down ter Wash'n'ton's plantation.' Ole Miss wuz a mighty smart woman, but she didn' know ev'ything.

"'Well,' says ole Marse, 'de craps'll be laid by in a mont' now, 'en den dey won't be much ter do fer ernudder mont' er six weeks. So we'll let her go down dere an' stay till cotton-pickin' time; I'll jes' len' 'er ter 'em till den. Ef dey wants ter keep 'er en' we finds we doan need 'er, den we'll talk furder 'bout sellin' 'er. We'll tell her dat we jes' gwine let her go down dere wid de chil'en a week er so en' den come back, en' den we won't hab no fuss 'bout it.'

"So dey fixed it dat erway, en' Cindy went off wid 'em, she 'spectin' ter be back in a week er so, en' de w'ite folks not hahdly 'lowin' she'd come back at all. Skundus didn' lack ter hab Cindy go, but he couldn' do nuthin'. He wuz wukkin' off in ernudder part er de plantation w'en she went erway, en' had ter tell her good-by de night befo'.

"Bimeby, w'en Cindy didn' come back in two or th'ee weeks, Skundus 'mence ter git res'less. En' Skundus wuz diff'ent f'um udder folks. Mos' folks w'en dey gits res'less can't sleep good, but de mo' res'lesser Skundus got, de mo! sleepier he 'peared ter git. W'eneber he wuz'n wukkin' ef eatin', he'd be sleepin'. Wen de yuther niggers 'ud be sky-larkin' 'roun' nights en' Sundays, Skundus 'ud be soun' asleep in his cabin. Things kep' on dis way fer 'bout a mont' atter Cindy went away, w'en one mawnin' Skundus didn't come ter wuk. Dey look' fer 'im 'roun' de plantation, but dey couldn' fin' 'im, en' befo' de day wuz gone, ev'ybody wuz sho' dat Skundus had runned erway.

"Cose dey wuz a great howdydo 'bout it. Nobody hadn' nebber runned erway fum Marse Dugal' befo', an' dey hadn' b'en a runaway nigger in de neighbo'hood fer th'ee er fo' years. De w'ite folks wuz all wukked up, en' dey wuz mo' ridin' er hosses en' mo' hitchin up er buggies d'n a little. Ole Marse Dugal' had a lot er papers printed en' stuck up on trees 'long de roads, en' dey wuz sump'n put in de noospapers—a free nigger fum down on de Wim'l'ton Road read de paper ter some er our ban's—tellin' all 'bout how high Skundus wuz, en' w'at kine er teef he had, en' 'bout a skyah he had on his lef cheek, en' how sleepy he wuz, en' off'rin' a reward er one hunder' dollars fer whoeber 'ud ketch 'im. But none of 'em eber cotch 'im.

"W'en Cindy fus' went away she wuz kinder down in de mouf fer a day er so. But she went to a fine new house, de folks treated her well en' dere wuz sich good comp'ny 'mongs' her own people, dat she made up 'er min' she might's well hab a good time fer de week er two she

wuz gwine ter stay down dere. But w'en de time roll' on en' she didn'
heared nothin' 'bout gwine back, she 'mence' ter git kinder skeered she
wuz'n nebber gwine ter see her mammy ner Skundus no mo'. She wuz
monst'us cut up 'bout it, an' los' 'er appetite en' got so po' en' skinny, her
mist'ess sont 'er down ter de swamp fer ter git some roots fer ter make
some tea fer 'er health. Her mist'ess sont her 'way 'bout th'ee o'clock en'
Cindy didn' come back till atter sundown; en' she say she b'en lookin' fer
de roots, dat dey didn' 'pear ter be none er dem kin' er roots fer a mile er
so 'long de aidge er de swamp.

"Cindy 'mence' ter git better jes' ez soon as she begun ter drink de
root-tea. It wuz a monst'us good med'cine, leas'ways in her case. It done
Cindy so much good dat her mist'ess 'eluded she'd take it herse'f en' gib
it ter de chil'en. De fus' day Cindy went atter de roots dey wuz some lef'
ober, en' her mist'ess tol' 'er fer ter use dat fer de nex' day. Cindy done so,
but she tol' 'er mist'ess hit didn' hab no strenk en' didn' do 'er no good.
So ev'y day atter dat Marse Wash'n'ton's wife 'ud sen' Cindy down by de
aidge er de swamp fer ter git fresh roots.

"'Cindy,' said one er de fiel'-han's one day, 'yer better keep 'way fum
dat swamp. Dey's a ha'nt walkin' down dere.'

"'Go way fum yere wid yo' foolishness,' said Cindy. 'Dey ain' no
ha'nts. W'ite folks doan' b'lieve in sich things, fer I heared 'em say so;
but yer can't 'spec' nothin' better fum fiel'-han's.'

"Dey wuz one man on de plantation, one er dese yer dandy niggers
w'at 'uz alluz runnin' atter de wimmen folks, dat got ter pest'rin' Cindy.
Cindy didn' paid no 'tention ter 'im, but he kep' on tryin' fer ter co't
her w'en he could git a chance. Fin'ly Cindy tole 'im fer ter let her
'lone, er e'se sump'n' might happen ter 'im. But he didn' min' Cindy,
en' one ebenin' he followed her down ter de swamp. He los' track un
er, en' ez he wuz a-startin' back out'n de swamp, a great big black
ha'nt 'bout ten feet high, en' wid a fence-rail in its ban's jump out'n de
bushes en' chase 'im cl'ar up in de co'n fiel'. Leas'ways he said it did; en'
atter dat none er de niggers wouldn't go nigh de swamp, 'cep'n Cindy,
who said it wuz all foolishness—it wuz dis nigger's guilty conscience
dat skeered 'im—she hadn' seed no ha'nt en' wuz'n skeered er nuffin'
she didn't see.

"Bimeby, w'en Cindy had be'n gone fum home 'bout two mont's,
harves'-time come on, en' Marse Dugal' foun' hisse'f short er ban's. One
er de men wuz down wid de rheumatiz, Skundus wuz gone, en' Cindy
wuz gone, en' Marse Dugal' tole ole Miss dey wuz no use talkin', he

couldn' 'ford ter buy no new ban's, en' he'd ha' ter sen' fer Cindy, 'en put her in de fiel'; fer de cotton-crap wuz a monst'us big 'un dat year, en' Cindy wuz one er de bes' cotton-pickers on de plantation. So dey wrote a letter to Marse Wash'n'ton dat day fer Cindy, en' wanted Cindy by de 'een er de mont', en' Marse Wash'n'ton sont her home. Cindy didn' 'pear ter wanter come much. She said she'd got kinder use' ter her noo home; but she didn' hab no mo' ter say 'bout comin' dan she did 'bout goin'. Howsomedever, she went down ter de swamp fer ter git roots fer her mist'ess up ter de las' day she wuz dere.

"Wen Cindy got back home, she wuz might'ly put out 'ca'se Skundus wuz gone, en' hit didn' 'pear ez ef anythin' anybody said ter 'er 'ud comfort 'er. But one mawnin' she said she'd dreamp' dat night dat Skundus wuz gwine ter come back; en' sho' 'nuff, de ve'y nex' mawnin' who sh'd come walkin' out in de fiel' wid his hoe on his shoulder but Skundus, rubbin' his eyes ez ef he hadn' got waked up good yit.

"Dey wuz a great 'miration mongs' de niggers, en' somebody run off ter de big house fer ter tell Marse Dugal'. Bimeby here come Marse Dugal' hisse'f, mad as a hawnit, acussin' en' gwine on like he gwine ter hurt somebody; but anybody w'at look close could' 'a' seed he wuz 'mos' tickled ter def fer ter git Skundus back ergin.

"'Whar yer be'n run erway ter, yer good-fer-nuthin', lazy, black nigger?' sez 'e. 'I'm gwine ter gib yer fo' hunderd lashes. I'm gwine ter hang yer up by yer thumbs en' take ev'y bit er yer black hide off'n yer, en' den I'm gwine ter sell yer ter de fus' specileter w'at comes' long buyin' niggers fer ter take down ter Alabam'. W'at yer mean by runnin' er way fum yer good, kin' marster, yer good-fer-nuthin', wool-headed, black scound'el?'

"Skundus looked at 'im ez ef he didn' understan'. 'Lawd, Marse Dugal',' sez 'e, 'I doan' know w'at youer talkin' 'bout. I ain' runned erway; I ain' be'n nowhar.'

"'Whar yer be'n fer de las' mon'?' said Marse Dugal'. 'Tell me de truf, er I'll hab yer tongue pulled out by de roots. I'll tar yer all ober yer en' set yer on fiah. I'll—I'll'—Marse Dugal' went on at a tarrable rate, but eve'ybody knowed Marse Dugal' bark uz wuss'n his bite.

"Skundus look lack 'e wuz skeered mos' ter def fer ter heah Marse Dugal' gwine on dat erway, en' he couldn' 'pear to un'erstan' w'at Marse Dugal' was talkin' erbout.

"'I didn' mean no harm by sleep'n in de barn las' night, Marse Dugal',' sez 'e, 'en' ef yer'll let me off dis time, I won' nebber do so no mo'.'

"Well, ter make a long story sho't, Skundus said he had gone ter de barn dat Sunday atternoon befo' de Monday w'en he could't be foun', fer ter hunt aigs, en' wiles he wuz up dere de hay had 'peared so sof en' nice dat he had laid down fer take a little nap; dat it wuz mawnin' w'en he woke en' foun' hisse'f all covered up whar de hay had fell over on 'im. A hen had built a nes' right on top un 'im, en' it had half-a-dozen aigs in it. He said he hadn't stop fer ter git no brekfus', but had jes' suck' one or two er de aigs en' hurried right straight out in de fiel', fer he seed it wuz late en' all de res' er de ban's wuz gone ter wuk.

"'Youer a liar,' said Marse Dugal', 'en' de truf ain't in yer. Yer b'en run erway en' hid in de swamp somewhar ernudder.' But Skundus swo' up en' down dat he hadn' b'en out'n dat barn, en' fin'lly Marse Dugal' went up ter de house en' Skundus went on wid his wuk.

"Well, yer mought know dey wuz a great 'miration in de neighbo'hood. Marse Dugal' sont fer Skundus ter cum up ter de big house nex' day, en' Skundus went up 'spect'n' fer ter ketch forty. But w'en he got dere, Marse Dugal' had fetched up ole Doctor Leach fum down on Rockfish, 'en another young doctor fum town, en' dey looked at Skundus's eyes en' felt of his wris' en' pulled out his tongue, en' hit 'im in de chis', en' put dey yeahs ter his side fer ter heah 'is heart beat; en' den dey up'n made Skundus tell how he felt w'en 'e went ter sleep en' how he felt w'en 'e woke up. Dey stayed ter dinner, en' w'en dey got thoo' talkin' en' eatin' en' drinkin', dey tole Marse Dugal' Skundus had had a catacornered fit, en' had be'n in a trance fer fo' weeks. En' w'en dey l'arned about Cindy, en' how dis yer fit had come on gradg'ly atter Cindy went away, dey 'lowed Marse Dugal' 'd better let Skundus en' Cindy git married, er he'd be liable ter hab some mo' er dem fits. Fer Marse Dugal' didn' want no fittified niggers ef 'e could he'p it.

"Atter dat, Marse Dugal' had Skundus up ter de house lots er times fer ter show 'im off ter folks w'at come ter visit. En' bein' as Cindy wuz back home, en' she en' Skundus wukked hahd, en' he couldn' 'ford fer ter take no chances on dem long trances, he 'lowed em ter got married soon ez cotton-pickin' wuz ober, en' gib 'em a cabin er dey own ter lib in down in de quarters. En' sho' 'nuff, dey didn' had no trouble keep'n' Skundus wak f'm dat time fo'th, fer Cindy turned out ter hab a temper of her own, en' made Skundus walk a chalk-line.

"Dis yer boy, Tom," said the old man, straightening out his leg carefully, preparatory to getting up, "is jes' like his gran'daddy. I b'lieve ef somebody didn' wake 'im up he'd sleep till jedgmen' day. Heah 'e comes now. Come on heah wid dat w'eelborrow, yer lazy, good-fer-nuthin' rascal."

Tom came slowly round the house with the wheelbarrow, and stood blinking and rolling his eyes as if he had just emerged from a sound sleep and was not yet half awake.

We took our way around the house, the ladies and I in front, Julius next and Tom bringing up the rear with the wheelbarrow. We went by the well-kept grape-vines, heavy with the promise of an abundant harvest, through a narrow field of yellowing corn, and then picked our way through the watermelon-vines to the spot where the monarch of the patch had lain the day before, in all the glory of its coat of variegated green. There was a shallow concavity in the sand where it had rested, but the melon itself was gone.

# LONESOME BEN

There had been some talk among local capitalists about building a cotton mill on Beaver Creek, a few miles from my place on the sand hills in North Carolina, and I had been approached as likely to take an interest in such an enterprise. While I had the matter under advisement it was suggested, as an inducement to my co-operation, that I might have the brick for the mill made on my place—there being clay there suitable for the purpose—and thus reduce the amount of my actual cash investment. Most of my land was sandy, though I had observed several outcroppings of clay along the little creek or branch forming one of my boundaries.

One afternoon in summer, when the sun was low and the heat less oppressive than it had been earlier in the day, I ordered Julius, our old colored coachman, to harness the mare to the rockaway and drive me to look at the clay-banks. When we were ready, my wife, who wished to go with me for the sake of the drive, came out and took her seat by my side.

We reached our first point of destination by a road running across the plantation, between a field of dark-green maize on the one hand and a broad expanse of scuppernong vines on the other. The road led us past a cabin occupied by one of my farm-hands. As the carriage went by at a walk, the woman of the house came to the door and curtsied. My wife made some inquiry about her health, and she replied that it was poor. I noticed that her complexion, which naturally was of a ruddy brown, was of a rather sickly hue. Indeed, I had observed a greater sallowness among both the colored people and the poor whites thereabouts than the hygienic conditions of the neighborhood seemed to justify.

After leaving this house our road lay through a cotton field for a short distance, and then we entered a strip of woods, through which ran the little stream beside which I had observed the clay. We stopped at the creek, the road by which we had come crossing it and continuing over the land of my neighbor, Colonel Pemberton. By the roadside, on my own land, a bank of clay rose in almost a sheer perpendicular for about ten feet, evidently extending back some distance into the low, pine-clad hill behind it, and having also frontage upon the creek. There were marks of bare feet on the ground along the base of the bank, and the face of it seemed freshly disturbed and scored with finger marks, as though children had been playing there.

"Do you think that clay would make good brick, Julius?" I asked the old man, who had been unusually quiet during the drive. He generally played with the whip, making little feints at the mare, or slapping her lightly with the reins, or admonishing her in a familiar way; but on this occasion the heat or some other cause had rendered him less demonstrative than usual.

"Yas, suh, I knows it would," he answered.

"How do you know? Has it ever been used for that purpose?"

"No, suh; but I got my reasons fer sayin' so. Ole Mars Dugal useter hab a brickya'd fu'ther up de branch—I dunno as yer noticed it, fer it's all growed ober wid weeds an' grass. Mars Dugal said dis yer clay wouldn' make good brick, but I knowed better."

I judged from the appearance of the clay that it was probably deficient in iron. It was of a yellowish-white tint and had a sort of greasy look.

"Well," I said, "we'll drive up to the other place and get a sample of that clay, and then we'll come back this way."

"Hold on a minute, dear," said my wife, looking at her watch, "Mabel has been over to Colonel Pemberton's all the afternoon. She said she'd be back at five. If we wait here a little while she'll be along and we can take her with us."

"All right," I said, "we'll wait for her. Drive up a little farther, Julius, by that jessamine vine."

While we were waiting, a white woman wearing a homespun dress and slat-bonnet, came down the road from the other side of the creek, and lifting her skirts slightly, waded with bare feet across the shallow stream. Reaching the clay-bank she stooped and gathered from it, with the aid of a convenient stick, a quantity of the clay which she pressed together in the form of a ball. She had not seen us at first, the bushes partially screening us; but when, having secured the clay, she turned her face in our direction and caught sight of us watching her, she hid the lump of clay in her pocket with a shamefaced look, and hurried away by the road she had come.

"What is she going to do with that, Uncle Julius?" asked my wife. We were Northern settlers, and still new to some of the customs of the locality, concerning which we often looked to Julius for information. He had lived on the place many years and knew the neighborhood thoroughly.

"She's gwineter eat it, Miss Annie," he replied, "w'en she gits outer sight."

"Ugh!" said my wife with a grimace, "you don't mean she's going to eat that great lump of clay?"

"Yas'm I does; dat's jes' w'at I means—gwineter eat eve'y bit un it, an' den come back bimeby fer mo'."

"I should think it would make them sick," she said.

"Dey gits use' ter it," said Julius. "Howsomeber, ef dey eats too much it does make 'em sick; an' I knows w'at I'm ertalkin' erbout. I doan min' w'at dem kinder folks does," he added, looking contemptuously after the retreating figure of the poor-white woman, "but w'eneber I sees black folks eat'n' clay of'n dat partic'lar clay-bank, it alluz sets me ter studyin' 'bout po' lonesome Ben."

"What was the matter with Ben?" asked my wife. "You can tell us while we're waiting for Mabel."

Old Julius often beguiled our leisure with stories of plantation life, some of them folk-lore stories, which we found to be in general circulation among the colored people; some of them tales of real life as Julius had seen it in the old slave days; but the most striking were, we suspected, purely imaginary, or so colored by old Julius's fancy as to make us speculate at times upon how many original minds, which might have added to the world's wealth of literature and art, had been buried in the ocean of slavery.

"W'en ole Mars Marrabo McSwayne owned dat place ober de branch dere, w'at Kunnel Pembe'ton owns now," the old man began, "he useter hab a nigger man name' Ben. Ben wuz one er dese yer big black niggers—he was mo'd'n six foot high an' black ez coal. He wuz a fiel'-han' an' a good wukker, but he had one little failin'—he would take a drap er so oncet in a w'ile. Co'se eve'ybody laks a drap now an' den, but it 'peared ter 'fec' Ben mo'd'n it did yuther folks. He didn' hab much chance dat-a-way, but eve'y now an' den he'd git holt er sump'n' somewahr, an' sho's he did, he'd git out'n de narrer road. Mars Marrabo kep' on wa'nin' 'm 'bout it, an' fin'lly he tol' 'im ef he eber ketch 'im in dat shape ag'in he 'uz gwineter gib 'im fo'ty. Ben knowed ole Mars Marrabo had a good 'memb'ance an' alluz done w'at he said, so he wuz monst'us keerful not ter gib 'm no 'casion fer ter use his 'memb'ance on him. An' so fer mos' a whole yeah Ben 'nied hisse'f an' nebber teched a drap er nuffin'.

"But it's h'ad wuk ter larn a ole dog new tricks, er ter make him fergit de ole uns, an' po' Ben's time come bimeby, jes' lak ev'ybody e'se's does. Mars Marrabo sent 'im ober ter dis yer plantation one day wid a bundle er cotton-sacks fer Mars Dugal',' an' wiles he wuz ober yere, de ole Debbil sent a' 'oman w'at had cas' her eyes on 'im an' knowed his weakness, fer ter temp' po' Ben wid some licker. Mars Whiskey wuz right dere an' Mars Marrabo wuz a mile erway, an' so Ben minded Mars Whiskey an' fergot 'bout Mars Marrabo. W'en he got back home he couldn' skasely tell Mars Marrabo de message w'at Mars Dugal' had sent back ter 'im.

"Mars Marrabo listen' at 'im 'temp' ter tell it; and den he says, kinder col' and cuttin'-like—he didn' 'pear ter get mad ner nuffin':

"'Youer drunk, Ben.'

"De way his marster spoke sorter sobered Ben, an' he 'nied it of co'se.

"'Who? Me, Mars Marrabo? I ain' drunk; no, marster, I ain' drunk. I ain' teched a drap er nuffin' sence las' Chris'mas, suh'.

"'Youer drunk, Ben, an' don't you dare ter 'spute my wo'd, er I'll kill you in yo' tracks! I'll talk ter you Sad'day night, suh, w'en you'll be sober, an' w'en you'll hab Sunday ter 'fleet over ou' conve'sation, an' 'nuss yo' woun's.'

"W'en Mars Marrabo got th'oo talkin' Ben wuz mo' sober dan he wuz befo' he got drunk. It wuz Wednesday w'en Ben's marster tol 'im dis, an' 'twix' den and Friday night Ben done a heap er studyin'. An' de mo' he studied de mo' he didn' lak de way Mars Marrabo talked. He hadn' much trouble wid Mars Marrabo befo',' but he knowed his ways, an' he knowed dat de longer Mars Marrabo waited to do a thing de; wusser he got 'stid er gittin' better lak mos' folks.' An' Ben fin'lly made up his min' he wa'n't gwineter take dat cow-hidin'. He 'lowed dat ef he wuz little, like some er de dahkies on de plantation, he wouldn' min' it so much; but he wuz so big dey'd be mo' groun' fer Mars Marrabo ter cover, an' it would hurt dat much mo'. So Ben 'cided ter run erway.

"He had a wife an' two chil'en, an' dey had a little cabin ter deyse'ves down in de quahters. His wife Dasdy wuz a good-lookin,' good-natu'd 'oman, an' 'peared ter set a heap er sto' by Ben. De little boy wuz name' Pete; he wuz 'bout eight er nine years ole, an' had already 'menced ter go out in de fiel' an' he'p his mammy pick cotton, fer Mars Marrabo wuz one er dese yer folks w'at wants ter make eve'y aidge cut. Dis yer little Pete wuz a mighty soople dancer, an' w'en his daddy would set out in de yahd an' pick de banjo fer 'im, Pete could teach de ole folks noo steps— dancin' jes seemed to come nachul ter 'im. Dey wuz a little gal too; Ben didn' pay much 'tention ter de gal, but he wuz monst'us fond er Dasdy an' de boy. He wuz sorry ter leab 'em, an' he didn' tell 'em nuffin' 'bout it fer fear dey'd make a fuss. But on Friday night Ben tuk all de bread an' meat dey wuz in de cabin an' made fer de woods.

"W'en Sad'day come an' Ben didn' 'pear, an' nobody didn' know nuffin' 'bout 'im, Mars Marrabo 'lowed of co'se dat Ben had runned erway. He got up a pahty an' tuk de dawgs out an' follered de scen' down ter de crick an' los' it. Fer Ben had tuk a go'd-full er tar 'long wid' 'im, an' w'en he got ter de crick he had 'n'inted his feet wid tar, an' dat th'owed de houns' off'n de scent. Dey sarched de woods an' follered de roads an' kep' watchin' fer a week, but dey couldn' fin' no sign er Ben. An' den Mars Marrabo got mo' stric', an' wuked his niggers hahder'n eber, ez ef he wanted ter try ter make up fer his loss.

"W'en Ben stahted out he wanted ter go ter de No'th. He didn' know how fur it wuz, bet he 'lowed he retch dar in fo' er five days. He knowed de No'th Stah, an' de fus night he kep' gwine right straight to'ds it. But de nex' night it was rainin,' an' fer two er th'ee nights it stayed cloudy, an' Ben couldn' see de No'th Stah. Howsomeber, he knowed he had got stahted right' an' he kep' gwine right straight on de same way fer a week er mo' 'spectin' ter git ter de No'th eve'y day, w'en one mawin' early, atter he had b'en walkin' all night, he come right smack out on de crick jes' whar he had stahted f'om.

"Co'se Ben wuz monst'us disapp'inted. He had been wond'rin' w'y he hadn' got ter de No'th befo',' an' behol,' heah he wuz back on de ole plantation. He couldn' un'erstan' it at fus,' but he wuz so hongry he didn' hab time ter study 'bout nuffin' fer a little w'ile but jes' ter git sump'n' ter eat; fer he had done eat up de bread an' meat he tuk away wid 'im, an' had been libbin' on roas'n-ears an' sweet'n taters he'd slip out'n de woods an' fin' in co'n fiel's 'an 'tater-patches. He look 'cross de crick, an' seed dis yer clay-bank, an' he waded ober an' got all he could eat, an' den tuk a lump wid 'im, an' hid in de woods ag'in 'til he could study de matter ober some.

"Fus' he 'lowed dat he better gib hiss'ef up an' take his lammin.' But jes' den he 'membered de way Mars Marrabo looked at 'im an' w'at he said 'bout Sad'day night; an' den he 'lowed dat ef Mars Marrabo ketch 'im now, he'd wear 'im ter a frazzle an' chaw up de frazzle, so de wouldn' be nuffin' lef' un 'im at all, an' dat Mars Marrabo would make a' example an' a warnin' of 'im fer all de niggers in de naberhood. Fac' is Mars Marrabo prob'ly wouldn' a' done much ter 'im fer it 'ud be monst'us po' 'couragement fer runaway niggers ter come back, ef dey gwineter git killed w'en dey come. An' so Ben waited 'til night, an' den he went back an' got some mo' clay an' eat it an' hid hisse'f in de woods ag'in.

"Well, hit wuz quare 'bout Ben, but he stayed roun' heah fer a mont,' hidin' in de woods in de daytime, an' slippin' out nights an' gittin' clay ter eat an' water f'om de crick yanker ter drink. De water in dat crick wuz cl'ar in dem days, stidder bein' yallar lak it is now."

We had observed that the water, like that of most streams that take their rise in swamps, had an amber tint to which the sand and clay background of the bed of the stream imparted an even yellower hue.

"What did he do then, Julius?" asked my wife, who liked to hear the end of a story.

"Well, Miss, he made up his min' den dat he wuz gwineter staht fer de No'th ag'in. But wiles he b'en layin' roun' in de woods he had 'mence ter feel monst'us lonesome, an' it 'peared ter him dat he jes' couldn' go widout seein' Dasdy an' little Pete. Fus' he 'lowed he'd go up ter de cabin, but he thought 'bout de dogs 'roun' de yahd, an' dat de yuther dahkies mought see 'im, and so he 'cided he'd better watch fer 'em 'til dey come long de road—it wuz dis yer same road—w'en he could come out'n de woods an' talk ter 'em. An' he eben 'lowed he mought 'suade 'em ter run erway wid 'im an' dey could all get ter de No'th, fer de nights wuz cl'ar now, an' he couldn' lose de No'th Stah.

"So he waited two er th'ee days, an' sho' nuff long come Dasdy one mornin,' comin' over to Mars Dugal's fer ter fetch some things fer her missis. She wuz lookin' kinder down in de mouf, fer she thought a heap er Ben, an' wuz monst'us sorry ter lose 'im, w'iles at de same time she wuz glad he wuz free, fer she 'lowed he'd done got ter de Norf long befo.' An' she wuz studyin' 'bout Ben, w'at a fine-lookin' man he wuz, an' wond'rin' ef she'd eber see 'im any mo.'

"W'en Ben seed her comin' he waited 'til she got close by, an' den he stepped out 'n de woods an' come face ter face wid her. She didn' 'pear to know who he wuz, an' seem kinder skeered.

"'Hoddy, Dasdy honey,' he said.

"'Huh!' she said, ''pears ter me you'er mighty fermilyer on sho't acquaintance.'

"'Sho't acquaintance.' Why, doan' yer know me, Dasdy?'

"'No. I doan know yer f'om a skeercrow. I never seed yer befo' in my life, an' nebber wants ter see yer ag'in. Whar did yer com f'om anyhow? Whose nigger is yer? Er is yer some low-down free nigger dat doan b'long ter nobody an' doan own nobody?'

"'W'at fer you talk ter me like dat, honey? I's Ben, yo' Ben. Why doan you know yo' own man?'

"He put out his ahms fer ter draw her ter 'im, but she jes' gib one yell, an' stahted ter run. Ben wuz so 'stonish' he didn' know w'at ter do, an' he stood dere in de road 'til he heared somebody e'se comin', w'en he dahted in de woods ag'in.

"Po' Ben wuz so 'sturbed in his min' dat he couldn' hahdly eat any clay dat day. He couldn' make out w'at wuz de matter wid Dasdy but he 'lowed maybe she'd heared he wuz dead er sump'n,' an' thought he wuz a ha'nt, an' dat wuz w'y she had run away. So he watch' by de side er de road, an' nex' mornin' who should come erlong but little Pete, wid a reed over his shoulder, an' a go'd-full er bait, gwine fishin' in de crick.

"Ben called 'im; 'Pete, O Pete! *Little* Pete.'

"Little Pete cocked up his ears an' listened. 'peared lak he'd heared dat voice befo.' He stahted fer de woods fer ter see who it wuz callin' 'im, but befo' he got dere Ben stepped out an' retched fer im.

"'Come heah, honey, an' see yo' daddy, who ain' seenyer fer so long.'

"But little Pete tuk one look at 'im, an' den 'menceter holler an squeal an' kick an' bite an' scratch. Ben wuz so 'stonish' dat he couldn' hoi' de boy, who slipped out'n his ban's an run to'ds de house ez fas' ez his legs would tote 'im.

"Po' Ben kep' gittin' wus an' wus mixed up. He couldn' make out fer de life er 'im w'at could be de matter. Nobody didn' 'pear ter wanter own 'im. He felt so cas' down dat he didn' notice a nigger man comin' long de road 'til he got right close up on 'im, an' didn' heah dis man w'en he said 'Hoddy' ter 'im.

"'Wat's de matter wid yer?' said de yuther man w'en Ben didn' 'spon'. 'Wat jedge er member er de legislater er hotel-keeper does you b'long ter dat you can't speak ter a man w'en he says hoddy ter yer?'

"Ben kinder come ter hisse'f an' seed it wuz Primus, who b'long ter his marster an' knowed 'im as well as anybody. But befo' he could git de words out'n his mouf Primus went on talkin.'

"'Youer de mos' mis'able lookin' merlatter I eber seed. Dem rags look lak dey be'n run th'oo a sawmill. My marster doan 'low no strange niggers roun' dis yer plantation, an' yo' better take yo' yaller hide 'way f'um yer as fas' as yo' kin.'

"Jes den somebody hollered on de yuther side er de crick, an' Primus stahted off on a run, so Ben didn' hab no chance ter say no mo' ter 'im.

"Ben almos' 'lowed he wuz gwine out'n' his min', he wuz so 'stonished an' mazed at none er dese yer folks reco'nizin' 'im. He went back in de woods ag'in an' stayed dere all day, wond'rin' w'at he wuz gwineter do. Oncet er twicet he seed folks comin' 'long de road, an' stahted out ter speak ter 'em, but changed his min' an' slip' back ag'in.

"Co'se ef Mars Marrabo had been huntin' Ben he would 'a' foun' 'im. But he had long sence los' all hope er seein' im ag'in, an' so nobody didn' 'sturb Ben in de woods. He stayed hid a day er two mo' an' den he got so lonesome an' homesick fer Dasdy an' little Pete an' de yuther dahkies,—somebody ter talk ter—dat he jes' made up his min' ter go right up ter de house an' gib hisse'f up an' take his med'cine. Mars Marrabo couldn' do nuffin' mo' d'n kill 'im an' he mought's well be dead as hidin' in de woods wid nobody ter talk ter er look at ner nuffin'. He had jes' come out 'n de woods an' stahted up dis ve'y road, w'en who sh'd come 'long in a hoss 'n buggy but ole Mars Marrabo, drivin' ober ter dat yuther brickyahd youer gwinter see now. Ben run out 'n de woods, and fell down on his knees in de road right in front er Mars Marrabo. Mars Marrabo had to pull on de lines an' hoi' de hoss up ter keep 'im f'um runnin' ober Ben.

"'Git out 'n de road, you fool nigger,' says Mars Marrabo, 'does yer wanter git run ober? Whose nigger is you, anyhow?'

"'I's yo' nigger, Mars Marrabo; doan yer know Ben, w'at runned erway?'

"'Yas, I knows my Ben w'at runned erway. Does you know whar he is?'

"'Why, I's yo' Ben, Mars Marrabo. Doan yer know me, marster?'

"'No, I doan know yer, yer yaller rascal! W'at de debbil yer mean by tellin' me sich a lie? Ben wuz black ez a coal an' straight ez an' arrer. Youer yaller ez dat clay-bank, an' crooked ez a bair'l-hoop. I reckon youer some 'stracted nigger, tun't out by some marster w'at doan wanter take keer er yer. You git off 'n my plantation, an' doan show yo' clay-cullud hide aroun' yer no more, er I'll hab yer sent ter jail an' whip.'

"Mars Marrabo drove erway an' lef' po' Ben mo' dead 'n alive. He crep' back in de bushes an' laid down an' wep' lak a baby. He didn' hab no wife, no chile, no frien's, no marster—he'd be'n willin' ernuff to git 'long widout a marster, w'en he had one, but it 'peared lak a sin fer his own marster ter 'ny 'im an' cas' 'im off dat-a-way. It 'peared ter 'im he mought jes' ez well be dead ez livin', fer he wuz all alone in de worl', wid nowhar ter go, an' nobody didn' hab nuffin' ter say ter 'im but ter 'buse 'im an' drive 'im erway.

"Atter he got ober his grievin' spell he 'mence ter wonder w'at Mars Marrabo meant by callin' 'im yaller, an' ez long ez nobody didn' seem ter keer whuther dey seed 'im er not, he went down by de crick in broad daylight, an' kneel down by de water an' looked at his face. Fus' he didn' reco'nize hisse'f an' glanshed back ter see ef dey wa'n't somebody lookin' ober his shoulder—but dey wa'n't. An' w'en he looked back in de water he seed de same thing—he wa'n't black no mo', but had turnt ter a light yaller.

"Ben didn' knowed w'at ter make er it fer a minute er so. Fus' he 'lowed he must hab de yaller fever, er de yaller janders, er sump'n lak dat'! But he had knowed rale dark folks ter hab janders befo', and it hadn't nebber 'fected 'em dat-a-way. But bimeby he got up o'ff'n 'is han's an' knees an' wuz stan'in' lookin' ober de crick at de clay-bank, an' wond'rin ef de clay he'd b'en eat'n' hadn' turnt 'im yaller w'en he heared sump'n say jes' ez plain ez wo'ds.

"'Turnt ter clay! turnt ter clay! turnt ter clay!'

"He looked all roun', but he couldn' see nobody but a big bullfrog settin' on a log on de yuther side er de crick. An' w'en he turnt roun' an' sta'ted back in de woods, he heared de same thing behin' 'im.

"'Turnt ter clay! turnt ter clay! turnt ter clay!'

"Dem wo'ds kep' ringin' in 'is yeahs 'til he fin'lly 'lowed dey wuz boun' ter be so, er e'se dey wouldn' a b'en tol ter 'im, an' dat he had libbed on clay so long an' had eat so much, dat he must 'a' jes nach'ly turnt ter clay!"

"Imperious Caesar, turned to clay, Might stop a hole to keep the wind away,"

I murmured parenthentically.

"Yas, suh," said the old man, "turnt ter clay. But you's mistook in de name, suh; hit wuz Ben, you 'member, not Caesar. Ole Mars Marrabo did hab a nigger name' Caesar, but dat wuz anudder one."

"Don't interrupt him, John," said my wife impatiently. "What happened then, Julius?"

"Well, po' Ben didn' know w'at ter do. He had be'n lonesome ernuff befo', but now he didn' eben hab his own se'f ter 'so'ciate wid, fer he felt mo' lak a stranger'n he did lak Ben. In a day er so mo' he 'mence ter wonder whuther he wuz libbin' er not. He had hearn 'bout folks turnin' ter clay w'en dey wuz dead, an' he 'lowed maybe he wuz dead an' didn' knowed it, an' dat wuz de reason w'y eve'body run erway f'm 'im an' wouldn' hab nuffin' ter do wid 'im. An' ennyhow, he 'lowed ef he wa'n't dead, he mought's well

CHARLES W. CHESNUTT

be. He wande'ed roun' a day er so mo', an' fin'lly de lonesomeness, an' de sleepin' out in de woods, 'mongs' de snakes an' sco'pions, an' not habbin' nuffin' fit ter eat, 'mence ter tell on him, mo' an' mo', an' he kep' gittin' weakah an' weakah 'til one day, w'en he went down by de crick fer ter git a drink er water, he foun' his limbs gittin' so stiff hit 'uz all he could do ter crawl up on de bank an' lay down in de sun. He laid dere 'til he died, an' de sun beat down on 'im, an' beat down on 'im, an' beat down on 'im, fer th'ee er fo' days, 'til it baked 'im as ha'd as a brick. An' den a big win' come erlong an' blowed a tree down, an' it fell on 'im an' smashed 'im all ter pieces, an' groun' 'im ter powder. An' den a big rain come erlong, an' washed 'im in de crick, 'an eber sence den de water in dat crick's b'en jes' as yer sees it now. An dat wuz de een' er po' lonesome Ben, an' dat's de reason w'y I knows dat clay'll make brick an' w'y I doan nebber lak ter see no black folks eat'n it."

My wife came of a family of reformers, who could never contemplate an evil without seeking an immediate remedy. When I decided that the bank of edible clay was not fit for brickmaking, she asked me if I would not have it carted away, suggesting at the same time that it could be used to fill a low place in another part of the plantation.

"It would be too expensive," I said.

"Oh, no," she replied, "I don't think so. I have been talking with Uncle Julius about it, and he says he has a nephew who is out of employment, and who will take the contract for ten dollars, if you will furnish the mule and cart, and board him while the job lasts."

As I had no desire to add another permanent member to my household, I told her it would be useless; that if the people did not get clay there they would find it elsewhere, and perhaps an inferior quality which might do greater harm, and that the best way to stop them from eating it was to teach them self-respect, when she had opportunity, and those habits of industry and thrift whereby they could get their living from the soil in a manner less direct but more commendable.

# Superstitions and Folk-Lore
## of the South

During a recent visit to North Carolina, after a long absence, I took occasion to inquire into the latter-day prevalence of the old-time belief in what was known as "conjuration" or "goopher," my childish recollection of which I have elsewhere embodied into a number of stories. The derivation of the word "goopher" I do not know, nor whether any other writer than myself has recognized its existence, though it is in frequent use in certain parts of the South. The origin of this curious superstition itself is perhaps more easily traceable. It probably grew, in the first place, out of African fetichism which was brought over from the dark continent along with the dark people. Certain features, too, suggest a distant affinity with Voodooism, or snake worship, a cult which seems to have been indigenous to tropical America. These beliefs, which in the place of their origin had all the sanctions of religion and social custom, became, in the shadow of the white man's civilization, a pale reflection of their former selves. In time, too, they were mingled and confused with the witchcraft and ghost lore of the white man, and the tricks and delusions of the Indian conjurer. In the old plantation days they flourished vigorously, though discouraged by the "great house," and their potency was well established among the blacks and the poorer whites. Education, however, has thrown the ban of disrepute upon witchcraft and conjuration. The stern frown of the preacher, who looks upon superstition as the ally of the Evil One; the scornful sneer of the teacher, who sees in it a part of the livery of bondage, have driven this quaint combination of ancestral traditions to the remote chimney corners of old black aunties, from which it is difficult for the stranger to unearth them. Mr. Harris, in his Uncle Remus stories, has, with fine literary discrimination, collected and put into pleasing and enduring form, the plantation stories which dealt with animal lore, but so little attention has been paid to those dealing with so-called conjuration, that they seem in a fair way to disappear, without leaving a trace behind. The loss may not be very great, but these vanishing traditions might furnish valuable data for the sociologist, in the future study of racial development. In writing, a few years ago, the volume entitled *The Conjure Woman*, I suspect that I was more influenced by the literary value of the material than by its sociological bearing, and therefore took, or thought I did, considerable liberty with my subject. Imagination, however, can only act upon data—one must have somewhere in his consciousness the ideas which he puts together to form a connected whole. Creative talent, of whatever grade, is, in the last analysis, only the power of rearrangement—there is nothing new under the sun. I was the more firmly impressed with this thought after I had interviewed half a dozen old women, and a genuine "conjure doctor;" for I discovered that the brilliant touches, due, I had thought, to my own imagination, were after all but dormant ideas, lodged in my childish mind by old Aunt This and old Uncle That, and awaiting only the spur of imagination to bring them again to the surface. For instance, in the story, "Hot-foot Hannibal," there figures a conjure doll with pepper feet. Those pepper feet I regarded as peculiarly my own, a purely original creation. I heard, only the other day, in North Carolina, of the consternation struck to the heart of a certain dark individual, upon finding upon his doorstep a rabbit's foot—a good omen in itself perhaps—to which a malign influence had been imparted by tying to one end of it, in the form of a cross, two small pods of red pepper!

Most of the delusions connected with this belief in conjuration grow out of mere lack of enlightenment. As primeval men saw a personality behind every natural phenomenon, and found a god or a devil in wind, rain, and hail, in lightning, and in storm, so the untaught man or woman who is assailed by an unusual ache or pain, some strenuous symptom of serious physical disorder, is prompt to accept the suggestion, which tradition approves, that some evil influence is behind his discomfort; and what more natural than to conclude that some rival in business or in love has set this force in motion?

Relics of ancestral barbarism are found among all peoples, but advanced civilization has at least shaken off the more obvious absurdities of superstition. We no longer attribute insanity to demoniac possession, nor suppose that a king's touch can cure scrofula. To many old people in the South, however, any unusual ache or pain is quite as likely to have been caused by some external evil influence as by natural causes. Tumors, sudden swellings due to inflammatory rheumatism or the bites of insects, are especially open to suspicion. Paralysis is proof positive of conjuration. If there is any doubt, the "conjure doctor" invariably removes it. The credulity of ignorance is his chief stock in trade—there is no question, when he is summoned, but that the patient has been tricked.

The means of conjuration are as simple as the indications. It is a condition of all witch stories that there must in some way be contact, either with the person, or with some object or image intended to represent the person to be affected; or, if not actual contact, at least close proximity. The charm is placed under the door-sill, or buried under the hearth, or hidden in the mattress of the person to be conjured. It may be a crude attempt to imitate the body of the victim, or it may consist merely of a bottle, or a gourd, or a little bag, containing a few rusty nails, crooked pins, or horsehairs. It may be a mysterious mixture thrown surreptitiously upon the person to be injured, or merely a line drawn across a road or path, which line it is fatal for a certain man or woman to cross. I heard of a case of a laboring man who went two miles out of his way, every morning and evening, while going to and from his work, to avoid such a line drawn for him by a certain powerful enemy.

Some of the more gruesome phases of the belief in conjuration suggest possible poisoning, a knowledge of which baleful art was once supposed to be widespread among the imported Negroes of the olden time. The blood or venom of snakes, spiders, and lizards is supposed to be employed for this purpose. The results of its administration are so peculiar, however, and so entirely improbable, that one is supposed to doubt even the initial use of poison, and figure it in as part of the same general delusion. For instance, a certain man "swelled up all over" and became "pieded," that is, pied or spotted. A white physician who was summoned thought that the man thus singularly afflicted was poisoned, but did not recognize the poison nor know the antidote. A conjure doctor, subsequently called in, was more prompt in his diagnosis. The man, he said, was poisoned with a lizard, which at that very moment was lodged somewhere in the patient's anatomy. The lizards and snakes in these stories, by the way, are not confined to the usual ducts and cavities of the human body, but seem to have freedom of movement throughout the whole structure. This lizard, according to the "doctor," would start from the man's shoulder, descend to his hand, return to the shoulder, and pass down the side of the body to the leg. When it reached the calf of the leg the lizard's head would appear right under the skin. After it had been perceptible for three days the lizard was to be cut out with a razor, or the man would die. Sure enough, the lizard manifested its presence in the appointed place at the appointed time; but the patient would not permit the surgery, and at the end of three days paid with death the penalty of his obstinacy. Old Aunt Harriet told me, with solemn earnestness, that she herself had taken a snake from her own arm, in sections, after a similar experience. Old Harriet may have been lying, but was, I imagine, merely self-deluded. Witches, prior to being burned, have often confessed their commerce with the Evil One. Why should Harriet hesitate to relate a simple personal experience which involved her in no blame whatever?

Old Uncle Jim, a shrewd, hard old sinner, and a palpable fraud, who did not, I imagine, believe in himself to any great extent, gave me some private points as to the manner in which these reptiles were thus transferred to the human system. If a snake or a lizard be killed, and a few drops of its blood be dried upon a plate or in a gourd, the person next eating or drinking from the contaminated vessel will soon become the unwilling landlord of a reptilian tenant. There are other avenues, too, by which the reptile may gain admittance; but when expelled by the conjure doctor's arts or medicines, it always leaves at the point where it entered. This belief may have originally derived its existence from the fact that certain tropical insects sometimes lay their eggs beneath the skins of animals, or even of men, from which it is difficult to expel them until the larvae are hatched. The chico or "jigger" of the West Indies and the Spanish Main is the most obvious example.

Old Aunt Harriet—last name uncertain, since she had borne those of her master, her mother, her putative father, and half a dozen husbands in succession, no one of which seemed to take undisputed precedence— related some very remarkable experiences. She at first manifested some reluctance to speak of conjuration, in the lore of which she was said to be well versed; but by listening patiently to her religious experiences— she was a dreamer of dreams and a seer of visions—I was able now and then to draw a little upon her reserves of superstition, if indeed her religion itself was much more than superstition.

"Wen I wuz a gal 'bout eighteen or nineteen," she confided, "de w'ite folks use' ter sen' me ter town ter fetch vegetables. One day I met a' ole conjuh man name' Jerry Macdonal, an' he said some rough, ugly things ter me. I says, says I, 'You mus' be a fool.' He didn' say nothin', but jes' looked at me wid 'is evil eye. Wen I come 'long back, dat ole man wuz stan'in' in de road in front er his house, an' w'en he seed me he stoop' down an' tech' de groun', jes' lack he wuz pickin' up somethin', an' den went 'long back in 'is ya'd. De ve'y minute I step' on de spot he tech', I felt a sha'p pain shoot thoo my right foot, it tu'n't under me, an' I fell down in de road. I pick' myself up an' by de time I got home, my foot wuz swoll' up twice its nachul size. I cried an' cried an' went on, fer I knowed I'd be'n trick' by dat ole man. Dat night in my sleep a voice spoke ter me an' says: 'Go an' git a plug er terbacker. Steep it in a skillet er wa'm water. Strip it lengthways, an' bin' it ter de bottom er yo' foot'.' I never didn' use terbacker, an' I laid dere, an' says ter myse'f, 'My Lawd, wa't is dat, wa't is dat!' Soon ez my foot got kind er easy, dat voice up an' speaks ag'in: 'Go an' git a plug er terbacker. Steep it in a skillet er wa'm water, an' bin' it ter de bottom er yo' foot.' I scramble' ter my feet, got de money out er my pocket, woke up de two little boys sleepin' on de flo', an' tol' 'em ter go ter de sto' an' git me a plug er terbacker. Dey didn' want ter go, said de sto' wuz shet, an' de sto' keeper gone ter bed. But I chased 'em fo'th, an' dey found' de sto' keeper an' fetch' de terbacker— dey sho' did. I soaked it in de skillet, an' stripped it 'long by degrees, till I got ter de en', w'en I boun' it under my foot an' roun' my ankle. Den I kneel' down an' prayed, an' next mawnin de swellin' wuz all gone! Dat voice wus de Spirit er de Lawd talkin' ter me, it sho' wuz! De Lawd have mussy upon us, praise his Holy Name!"

Very obviously Harriet had sprained her ankle while looking at the old man instead of watching the path, and the hot fomentation had reduced the swelling. She is not the first person to hear spirit voices in his or her own vagrant imaginings.

On another occasion, Aunt Harriet's finger swelled up "as big as a corn cob." She at first supposed the swelling to be due to a felon. She went to old Uncle Julius Lutterloh, who told her that some one had tricked her. "My Lawd!" she exclaimed, "how did they fix my finger?" He explained that it was done while in the act of shaking hands. "Doctor" Julius opened the finger with a sharp knife and showed Harriet two seeds at the bottom of the incision. He instructed her to put a poultice of red onions on the wound over night, and in the morning the seeds would come out. She was then to put the two seeds in a skillet, on the right hand side of the fire-place, in a pint of water, and let them simmer nine mornings, and on the ninth morning she was to let all the water simmer out, and when the last drop should have gone, the one that put the seeds in her hand was to go out of this world! Harriet, however, did not pursue the treatment to the bitter end. The seeds, once extracted, she put into a small phial, which she corked up tightly and put carefully away in her bureau drawer. One morning she went to look at them, and one of them was gone. Shortly afterwards the other disappeared. Aunt Harriet has a theory that she had been tricked by a woman of whom her

CHARLES W. CHESNUTT

husband of that time was unduly fond, and that the faithless husband had returned the seeds to their original owner. A part of the scheme of conjuration is that the conjure doctor can remove the spell and put it back upon the one who laid it. I was unable to learn, however, of any instance where this extreme penalty had been insisted upon.

It is seldom that any of these old Negroes will admit that he or she possesses the power to conjure, though those who can remove spells are very willing to make their accomplishment known, and to exercise it for a consideration. The only professional conjure doctor whom I met was old Uncle Jim Davis, with whom I arranged a personal interview. He came to see me one evening, but almost immediately upon his arrival a minister called. The powers of light prevailed over those of darkness, and Jim was dismissed until a later time, with a commission to prepare for me a conjure "hand" or good luck charm, of which, he informed some of the children about the house, who were much interested in the proceedings. I was very much in need. I subsequently secured the charm, for which, considering its potency, the small sum of silver it cost me was no extravagant outlay. It is a very small bag of roots and herbs, and, if used according to directions, is guaranteed to insure me good luck and "keep me from losing my job." The directions require it to be wet with spirits nine mornings in succession, to be carried on the person, in a pocket on the right hand side, care being taken that it does not come in contact with any tobacco. When I add that I procured, from an equally trustworthy source, a genuine graveyard rabbit's foot, I would seem to be reasonably well protected against casual misfortune. I shall not, however, presume upon this immunity, and shall omit no reasonable precaution which the condition of my health or my affairs may render prudent.

An interesting conjure story, which I heard, involves the fate of a lost voice. A certain woman's lover was enticed away by another woman, who sang very sweetly, and who, the jilted one suspected, had told lies about her. Having decided upon the method of punishment for this wickedness, the injured woman watched the other closely, in order to find a suitable opportunity for carrying out her purpose; but in vain, for the fortunate one, knowing of her enmity, would never speak to her or remain near her. One day the jilted woman plucked a red rose from her garden, and hid herself in the bushes near her rival's cabin. Very soon an old woman came by, who was accosted by the woman in hiding, and requested to hand the red rose to the woman of the house.

The old woman, suspecting no evil, took the rose and approached the house, the other woman following her closely, but keeping herself always out of sight. When the old woman, having reached the door and called out the mistress of the house, delivered the rose as requested, the recipient thanked the giver in a loud voice, knowing the old woman to be somewhat deaf. At the moment she spoke, the woman in hiding reached up and caught her rival's voice, and clasping it tightly in her right hand, escaped unseen, to her own cabin. At the same instant the afflicted woman missed her voice, and felt a sharp pain shoot through her left arm, just below the elbow. She at first suspected the old woman of having tricked her through the medium of the red rose, but was subsequently informed by a conjure doctor that her voice had been stolen, and that the old woman was innocent. For the pain he gave her a bottle of medicine, of which nine drops were to be applied three times a day, and rubbed in with the first two fingers of the right hand, care being taken not to let any other part of the hand touch the arm, as this would render the medicine useless. By the aid of a mirror, in which he called up her image, the conjure doctor ascertained who was the guilty person. He sought her out and charged her with the crime which she promptly denied. Being pressed, however, she admitted her guilt. The doctor insisted upon immediate restitution. She expressed her willingness, and at the same time her inability to comply—she had taken the voice, but did not possess the power to restore it. The conjure doctor was obdurate and at once placed a spell upon her which is to remain until the lost voice is restored. The case is still pending, I understand; I shall sometime take steps to find out how it terminates.

How far a story like this is original, and how far a mere reflection of familiar wonder stories, is purely a matter of speculation. When the old mammies would tell the tales of Br'er Rabbit and Br'er Fox to the master's children, these in turn would no doubt repeat the fairy tales which they had read in books or heard from their parents' lips. The magic mirror is as old as literature. The inability to restore the stolen voice is foreshadowed in the *Arabian Nights*, when the "Open Sesame" is forgotten. The act of catching the voice has a simplicity which stamps it as original, the only analogy of which I can at present think being the story of later date, of the words which were frozen silent during the extreme cold of an Arctic winter, and became audible again the following summer when they had thawed out.

CHARLES W. CHESNUTT

# A Note About the Author

Charles W. Chesnutt (1858–1932) was an African American author, lawyer, and political activist. Born in Cleveland to a family of "free persons of color" from North Carolina, Chesnutt spent his youth in Ohio before returning to the South after the Civil War. As a teenager, he worked as a teacher at a local school for Black students and eventually became principal at a college established in Fayetteville for the purpose of training Black teachers. Chesnutt married Susan Perry—with whom he had four daughters—in 1878 and moved to New York City for a short time before settling in Cleveland, where he studied law and passed the bar exam in 1887. His story "The Goophered Grapevine," published the same year, was the first story by an African American to appear in *The Atlantic*. Back in Ohio, Chesnutt started the court stenography business that would earn him the financial stability to pursue a career as a writer. He wrote several collections of short stories, including *The Conjure Woman* (1899) and *The Wife of His Youth and Other Stories of the Color-Line* (1899), both of which explore themes of race in America and African American identity as well as employ African American Vernacular English. Chesnutt was also an active member of the NAACP throughout his life, writing for its magazine *The Crisis*, serving on its General Committee, and working with such figures as W.E.B. Du Bois and Booker T. Washington.

# A Note from the Publisher

Spanning many genres, from non-fiction essays to literature classics to children's books and lyric poetry, Mint Edition books showcase the master works of our time in a modern new package. The text is freshly typeset, is clean and easy to read, and features a new note about the author in each volume. Many books also include exclusive new introductory material. Every book boasts a striking new cover, which makes it as appropriate for collecting as it is for gift giving. Mint Edition books are only printed when a reader orders them, so natural resources are not wasted. We're proud that our books are never manufactured in excess and exist only in the exact quantity they need to be read and enjoyed. To learn more and view our library, go to minteditionbooks.com

# bⱰⱭkfinity &  MINT EDITIONS

Enjoy more of your favorite classics with Bookfinity,
a new search and discovery experience for readers.
With Bookfinity, you can discover more vintage
literature for your collection, find your Reader Type,
track books you've read or want to read,
and add reviews to your favorite books.
Visit www.bookfinity.com, and click on
Take the Quiz to get started.

Don't forget to follow us
@bookfinityofficial and @mint_editions

CPSIA information can be obtained
at www.ICGtesting.com
Printed in the USA
LVHW051702010721
691689LV00014B/770